I0724769

SMALL FOREST

Spineless Wonders
ABN98156041888
PO Box 220 STRAWBERRY HILLS
New South Wales, Australia, 2012
www.shortaustralianstories.com.au

First published by Spineless Wonders 2019

Text copyright © William Lane 2018
Cover design by Bettina Kaiser.
Editorial Assistant, Bridgette Sulicich. Layout, Bronwyn Mehan.

All rights reserved. Without limiting the rights under copyright reserved above, no part of this publication may be produced, stored in or introduced into a retrieval sysem, or transmitted, in any form or by any means (electronic, mechanical, photocopying, recording or otherwise) without the prior written permission of the publisher of this book.

Typeset in Adobe Garamond Pro

National Library of Australia
Small Forest/ William Lane
1st ed.
ISBN 978-1-925052-41-1

A823.4

A catalogue record for this book is available from the National Library of Australia

This project has been assisted by the Copyright Agency Cultural Fund.

COPYRIGHT AGENCY
CULTURAL FUND

SMALL FOREST

WILLIAM LANE

Contents

The New World	9
The Children's Hospital	17
Uncle Dan's War	33
Vivien's Fingers	53
The Glider	69
Love	83
Eternal Rose	97
New Sound Recording	105
The Tree Line	119
Previous Publications	155
Biography	157

The New World

In autumn she would always remember the old world. The air was thinner in autumn. The spaces between the houses grew. The leaves deepened and turned bitter colours. Dora pulled the cardigan about her, and stood by the kitchen sink, staring into the morning of the garden. Her toast and tea grew cold.

In the street letterboxes sprouted like mushrooms. She could see windows once hidden by leaves.

Then Dora heard what she had been waiting for – singing: a thin, high voice, the frailest voice of a girl, singing in the street. The singing drew closer. The tendril of song wavered, trembled, then caught around her heart. She knew this song.

The girl passed by, head down, on her way to school, watching her shoes *shuck shuck shuck* the fallen leaves.

Dora quickly took up her purse and closed the door behind her. She began following the song down the street.

Still singing, the girl had cut across the park, leaving footsteps in the wet grass. Dora followed. They passed the swings and see-saws beaded with little tears of dew. Dora's heart drummed, intent on the line of melody the girl trailed. The song was unstitching Dora note by note. She was unfurling beneath a different sky than this, the northern sky of her childhood.

The girl passed through the school gate. The song faded as she climbed the school path, then was silenced behind glass.

Dora stood for a moment, as the melody went on in her mind. There was more of it, she knew, just beyond her memory. The girl always sang the beginning of the song, but never the end.

Opposite the school gates stood the New World supermarket.

Dora took heart. She would do some shopping. She stroked the once furry sides of her purse. She must not cry, although she still could not find the end of the song.

Before crossing the street, she looked up; in this place the sky was so high, so blue.

She headed towards the arcade neighbouring the New World. She would go to the butcher's first. Skint the butcher would be giving the finishing touches to arranging the meat in his shop window. He did it so artfully, as if the different cuts meant different things to him.

The doors to the arcade opened, responding to the pressure of Dora's little leading foot. Inside she smelt the ink and ammonia of the newsagent and the doctor's surgery. These scents warmed her. These were the smells of shelter, of the metropolis, of order. And as the doors closed, she had the sensation of her back being covered, and the shutting out of the sky.

The automatic door to the doctor's surgery hastened to open as she passed. An antiseptic slice of interior wafted into the arcade. Dora, who was approaching the age of strokes, averted her face, and pushed open the door of Skint's.

She might be the first customer. Skint the butcher stood in the shallow neon light with his back to the counter, repeatedly hacking at a side of beef – rather lacklustrely, thought Dora; *desultory*, perhaps that was the word. Almost like a schoolboy pelting a tree or a body of water. Was Skint unwell? Becoming aware of a customer's presence, Skint turned, and came shuffling to serve, the way the old butchers do. The tools of his trade, clustered on his thigh, jangled and padded.

'Ah, Mrs Lamb,' said Skint, wiping his palms, 'what can I do for you today?'

Dora surveyed the exhibited meat, and licked her lips.

The butcher's hands were dyed pink, and bunched like frankfurters. They seemed so blurred, so numb, Dora wondered if they were capable of feeling. Or touching.

'Cold outside?' enquired Skint.

'Oh, I was born in a colder country than this, Mr Skint.'

'I don't feel the cold neither.'

'Do they suffer?'

'Mrs Lamb?'

'Do the animals suffer?'

'I can assure you, Mrs Lamb, the process is quick, quick and painless. They don't feel a thing.'

Skint clasped his hands afresh and tucked in his chin. 'They don't feel a thing,' the butcher repeated. His heavily-lidded eyes travelled towards the shop window.

Dora's followed. People were walking hurriedly beyond the glass, head-down. A thread of melody like a nerve was running back through her mind. Bells jingled in the stalls of a market. Cattle lowed and steamed. Hooves and feet stamped, whips cracking. The long, luxurious morning pisses of the cattle. Who don't feel a thing.

'Sometimes I see them, you know,' said Dora, 'at night – the cattle trucks. Full of cattle. Do they only transport them at night? The stench of it. I remember it. I remembered it from when I was a girl. And not only cows. Not only – cows.'

The butcher wiped red hands back and forth on his apron. He began whistling. Killing time.

Dora suddenly turned and made for the door. She pushed and pushed – it would not open. She began shaking it violently. Skint was talking to her, advising her over the counter, but she could not hear, her ears were full of other sounds. He had to come around from behind the counter, and open the door for her – it only needed a pull, not a push – before she could flee, and gasp in unbutchered air, where she became a little girl again, watching the cows being slaughtered. No, not the cows – although she had seen that – but a man – a man at the head of a line of men. Now she remembered the song the school girl had been singing, from beginning to end. The men had been singing it, in unison, before the wall behind turned red, and their souls hovered level with the thatch in a group.

Then right before her, in the middle of the arcade, a child was crying, turning, its face drawn and crimson, distended in despair.

'It's crying!' exclaimed Dora.

'What of it?' snapped an approaching woman, who identified herself as the mother by walking to the child and hitting it. The woman's shopping bags slid along her arm, pummeling the child one by one. The child's mouth opened and shut.

'And it's suffering!' cried Dora, kneeling.

'It's doing no such thing,' shouted the woman, now looking frightened. 'Don't touch my child!'

The child was dragged off across ox-blood tiles, leaving Dora kneeling with arms akimbo. She rose, shook her head, took an uncertain step, and was ushered back into the car park by those nervously obliging doors.

Across the tops of the cars, a children's choir distantly sang in one of the school buildings. Joining other voices in twilight, over dark sloping fields. High girls' voices, harmonising without thought, moving as a body across the harvested land, as Dora shuffled across the car park, making towards the New World – where another set of automatic doors hurriedly opened onto tinselly, trebly music. Dora proceeded directly to the Frozen Goods. She liked freezing things. Then the Canned Goods, every day she bought more canned goods, they lasted years.

She bought as much as she could carry.

In the confectionary aisle she realised the ancient melody in her head had been buried under piped pop music, and she could not remember it if she tried.

Dora felt better. Outside the sun was beginning to warm the car park, beginning to blind. *I should apologise to Mr Skint right now*, she thought, *I'll have to face him sooner or later. It's always wise to be on good terms with your butcher. Your meat depends on it.*

'Ah! Mrs Lamb,' said Skint, much as he had previously. 'Bit of a turn? Feeling better I hope?'

Skint dolefully regarded his contrite customer.

'Yes, thank you,' admitted Dora, flushing, 'I feel so much better now. I must apologise for earlier. I wasn't myself. Now, can I have a look at that rack of lamb?'

Skint sheathed his knife. He took up the cleaver and brought her an eight-fingered side. 'I been saving you this one,' he confided.

Dora inspected the fatty margins laced with vessels, mentally testing the texture of the meat and the webby intervals between the bone.

'Yes, it does look lovely,' she admitted, 'thank you, Mr Skint. I'll take it.'

Skint sliced off some of the fat, whistling brightly, and Dora found herself tapping her fingertips to the tune.

The Children's Hospital

It took Tina some time to realise what was wrong with the children. She heard them whisper from their beds in the night. She heard them discussing the hospital food in meticulous detail. Then she heard them vomiting in the toilets.

At first Tina could not take it in – she could only attend to her child. He was quite a different case. A little boy of two, Peter had contracted a form of blood poisoning. Tina knew one in ten children died of this condition. She knew that, but felt by concentrating all her powers upon Peter she could prevent this happening. When a doctor put a needle in the little boy's spine (four nurses holding him down) and drew out a syringe of spinal fluid, she saw it was not cloudy. That was good.

But that had been three days before, and the medical team had not yet found the correct antibiotic to combat this particular strain of the infection. Not yet. The team was growing.

So Peter lay connected to a drip in a ward of the children's hospital and slowly worsened, while Tina waited. It was the best place the boy could be, Tina's husband assured her. Well, the best under the circumstances, he meant. He had told her that on his first and only visit.

Henry, the boy in the bed beside Peter, was probably eleven or twelve, although it was hard to tell. He spoke like a university student, yet his body was stick-like and undeveloped. Before, during and after every meal Henry swapped dietary and culinary notes with Amanda, the girl in the bed opposite. Amanda was also eleven or twelve, fair and skeletal, with tissue-paper skin. In appearance she was not unlike Henry.

'Did you get chicken?' Henry would ask, peering across the little ward.

'Yes.'

'How much?'

'Eighty grams.'

'I got ninety. That's not fair.'

'Did you get biscuits?'

'Yes.'

'Two coffee biscuits with sugar on top?'

'Mine are Iced VoVos.'

'Arnott's? Or an imitation brand?'

In whispers the children began proposing swaps and various deals – your biscuit for my apple.

One morning Henry's mother came to sit by her son's bed. Tina met the woman's eyes, and saw they were frantic beneath the surface. They must have been frantic for months, for years now, those eyes, thought Tina. Wanting to give the mother and child a little privacy, Tina decided to walk about the hospital, if only for a few minutes. Peter was asleep; his temperature was stable.

But when she returned she found Peter had worsened suddenly, the way children do – plummeting into illness, soaring into wellbeing. The little boy tugged at the cannula in his sleep, where a blood ring with plasma satellites seeped through the securing tape. *I shouldn't have left him, shouldn't have left him,* was all Tina could think, sponging Peter's head from a bowl of water that soon grew warm.

Tina's mother arrived, a short, rotund, Arabic-speaking woman with a tragic air, forever bearing food.

'He needs food,' Grandma declared, pinching Peter's legs. 'See, he's losing weight. I've brought him his favourite biscuits.'

'He can't eat, Mum!' replied Tina, trying not to raise her voice. 'You know that.'

'He needs to eat–'

'Mum!'

The homely smell of Grandma's cooking began permeating the ward. Amanda in the bed opposite wrinkled her nose, and she frowned at the television bolted to the roof above her bed.

'But he's getting thin,' insisted Grandma.

'Do you think I don't notice he's thin'? But he's on a drip – see? He's getting all he needs. Let go of his leg – don't wake him!'

'He's not thin. He's fat,' said Amanda from the bed opposite.

Grandma shrugged, palms upward. Then she looked at Henry's immaculately-made bed, and clucked approvingly. Henry had gone for a short walk with his mother. Grandma, who had taken Henry under her wing, placed a plate of baklava on the foot of the smooth bed.

'Mum, what are you doing putting food on Henry's bed?' asked Tina.

'It's what he needs. I thought he might like my baklava. It's the best ingredients.'

'Mum, Henry is a very sick boy. He can't eat baklava. It's far too rich. Your baklava would probably kill Henry.'

Amanda glared from across the room at the plate occupying Henry's bed.

'He needs fattening up,' said Grandma. 'The poor boy is skin and bone.'

At that moment Henry appeared in the doorway. Still dressed in his pyjamas (the children never changed out of their pyjamas), his hair ruffled, Henry paused warily.

'Your friend's here,' commented Amanda.

Henry frowned at the plate of baklava swimming in honey on his bed. The baklava was odourless – but not so Grandma's tabouli, which had done battle with the antiseptic smell of the ward, and completely overwhelmed it. Suddenly the boy gagged, running away down the corridor.

'Look what you did to him, Mum!'

'What is wrong with these children?' cried Grandma, throwing up her arms, arms round and white in her black dress. 'I don't understand – all these beautiful blond children, starving to death. Are they ghosts?'

'They won't eat.'

'Won't eat? Children who won't eat? Whoever heard of such a thing? Tina, you ate like a horse, all my children ate like horses.'

'Mum!'

A nurse took Peter's temperature, impervious to the shots of Arabic fired across the bed. The boy's temperature was still very high. Not brain-damage high, but seriously high. Grandma began quizzing Tina what the temperature really meant. Tina walked away, trying not to scream.

Later that day, Tina came upon Henry and Amanda hunched together in the corridor, conferring with a third apparition of a child, Penny.

'How much chicken did you get the night before last, Penny?' whispered Henry.

'Eighty grams.'

'Why was I given ninety?' asked Henry, 'when you both got eighty?'

'Maybe they knew we'd have this conversation,' said Penny.

The three children looked covertly towards the nurses' station.

Penny occupied a room by herself. She was a fevered-looking child, eyes bright and sunken, cheeks hollow. She shuffled about in slippers wheeling a drip inserted in her stick of an arm. One of the nurses had told Tina that Penny had been a resident in the ward over a year. 'A year!' Tina had exclaimed. 'That's nothing,' the nurse confided, 'you haven't seen the ones upstairs.

They've been there for*ever*. They haven't eaten for *years.*' Penny had requested to be moved from Henry and Amanda's ward, according to the nurse, because she was too frightened to be in the same room as Amanda, especially at night.

'Eat your chicken?' Amanda asked Penny.

'About seventy grams.'

'You're not going to get your pass out. You know that, don't you.'

'That's none of your beeswax. Don't tell me what to eat. You can talk. I heard you chucking up ten minutes ago. You can't even eat a scoop of ice cream without chucking up. You'll be going upstairs soon.'

'You've been snooping in the toilets again.'

'Stop it girls,' scolded Henry. 'Did you know a pear has more calories than a peach?'

'You're not thinking of the GI?'

'Of course not.'

'How many calories do apples have?'

'With or without the skin?'

Big or small. Green or red. Sundowners or Red Delicious.

That night, sleeping on a cot beside Peter's bed, Tina started awake to see a pale head floating above them. It was Henry. Across the room Amanda watched, big-eyed.

'I think Peter's getting better,' said Henry the next morning, sitting up in bed while reading the last pages of *The Brothers Karamazov*.

'I think so too,' said Tina. 'He turned the corner in the night, although I hardly dare say it.'

The doctor on the morning rounds confirmed it; yes, the new antibiotic was working.

Tina could not stop stroking Peter's back, to feel how cool it ran.

'Are you doing your school work?' she asked Henry. She was curious that he was reading Dostoyevsky.

'I've done it already. I only do about an hour in the morning and I still come top. Could you thank your mum for the food she brought yesterday? Tell her I'm sorry but I couldn't eat it. I'm only allowed to eat what they tell me to eat. They watch us pretty closely in here.'

'Why don't you mention it to her yourself?'

'But you might have left by the time she visits again.'

'I wish!'

Then Tina bit her lip. Amanda laughed.

'Do you know when you are going?' Henry asked. 'Sorry, that's rude to ask, isn't it.'

'It's alright, Henry,' Tina answered. 'No, I don't know when we're going. I'll tell you as soon as I find out. I think it will be some days yet.'

'Oh, I expect I'll find out before you,' said Henry. 'People come and go. I've seen dozens of people in that bed. They always get better, and then they go. Where is your husband?'

'He's busy,' answered Tina, startled by the question.

'Lots of people don't like coming here,' said Henry, returning to Dostoyevsky.

'It's not that.'

'I wasn't saying it was so in your husband's case.'

Amanda's father appeared and sat by her bed. His manner was expensive, accustomed to results, boardroom. Amanda flicked through channels.

'I've bought you a book,' the father said.

Amanda pointed the remote at him, and pressed 'off', first with a small downwards movement, then a sudden upwards movement.

Tina left the ward again.

She wandered the wings of the children's hospital, past shops, telephones, ATMs, newsagents, cafés, a chapel, a library – and art, such a fine collection of art, a Nolan outside Radiology, a Whiteley by Burns. The architecture so airy and sheer, creating an atmosphere of light, weightlessness, freedom.

In the distance, through great panes of glass, cars beetled past neat suburban gardens.

For the first time in days Tina ventured into the fresh air, crossing a courtyard of plastic tables and chairs. Support staff in white or blue uniforms smoked furtively, warming themselves in the winter sun. Tina was surprised to discover it was morning. It seemed strange that mornings still occurred, that the sun still shone, that life had been continuing beyond the children's hospital. She walked on through the large grounds. There was Henry, wandering beside his mother. The couple passed slowly by the flowerbeds, like two privately close siblings. A little later Tina heard coughing, retching. It was Henry near the hospital wishing well, his head in a hedge, his shoulders rising and falling.

Henry watched over Peter. He wheeled the little boy's drip when Peter left the bed and explored the corridor for the first time. He tickled Peter's feet. Every day he said, 'He's putting on weight.'

Tina could not see it, but when the nurse weighed Peter, Henry was right.

Once in the morning and once in the afternoon, Penny appeared in the doorway, like a little headmistress scrutinising a dormitory. Her gaze lingered on the least alteration to the ward. 'What are you staring at?' Amanda would say. 'Looking for your boyfriend?' Penny would ignore the sprite, moving off in her own time – but slowly, stiffly, tagged by her drip.

Amanda ignored almost everyone – nurses, social workers, psychologists, psychiatrists, paediatricians, dieticians, physiotherapists, occupational therapists, wards-men, cleaners, tea ladies, clowns, parents, Tina and Grandma, even little Peter. She would only talk to Henry, or, when she could possibly rile her, Penny.

'I don't know how Amanda can lie there watching TV all the time,' Henry once confided to Tina while Amanda was in the toilet. 'I hate the ads. I despise advertisements. They represent everything that's wrong with this world. I hate the voice they put on in ads. How that voice pretends the world is – that's what I hate. What that voice has learnt it can safely assume – that's what makes me sick.' Then Henry went back to reading *Our Mutual Friend*. He had a special stand with an adjustable arm to support his heavy reading matter.

Grandma visited every day, never failing to offer Henry a new dish. She needed to find a food he could eat, some key dish he could not resist – the elixir, the manna that would restore Henry. After a week he did try a crust of Lebanese pastry, but grew immediately pale, and, smiling feebly, pushed aside the plate.

'Eat, Henry, *eat*!' urged Grandma in her guttural English.

'Mum!' cried Tina.

'Henry must eat! *Eat*!'

Grandma was right of course. Tina heard it confirmed that night, after the lights went out: 'Amanda? Did you get your pass out?' Henry whispered. Before this whispering, the children always waited until they thought Tina was asleep.

'I got it,' said Amanda, 'I made sure I got it.'

'You tricked them?'

Amanda did not answer.

'Is it a two hour pass or a four?' asked Henry.

'Two.'

'Where will you go? Who will you go with? When are you going?' Then, in an even more hushed voice, Henry asked, 'How much were you?'

'Thirty-three kilos and eight hundred grams. You?'

'Thirty-four and two hundred.'

'You've lost half,' said Amanda.

'I know.'

'That's dangerous.'

'I'm still heavier than you.'

'You're a boy.'

'I'm younger than you,' said Henry.

'It's still serious, Henry. You'll be upstairs soon. That's what Penny said.'

'I don't care what Penny said. I know you two talk about me behind my back.'

'She might be going upstairs,' said Amanda.

'Penny? Who said?'

'What does it matter who said?'

'Of course it matters,' said Henry. 'No-one can send her upstairs except the senior doctor.'

'So you're now thirty-four and a quarter. Less.'

After a silence Henry whispered, 'Surprised they gave us cake again?'

'Two nights in a row. What do you think they are up to?'

'Good news,' announced the doctor to Tina the next day, 'Peter can go home today.'

Tina could not help glancing at Henry. He had seemed standoffish that morning. He lay on his bed fixedly reading *Jane Eyre*.

Grandma appeared with her granddaughter, Mona. Mona was a plump girl with an already ample belly protruding between her stretched top and tummy-tight shorts. Her swarthy skin radiated, she might have bounced in straight from the beach – in fact, she had. Mona stood by Peter's bed and consumed a large cookie. The cookie crinkled as she pushed it up from its plastic packaging. Crumbs and chocolate chips strewed on the floor. With each falling piece Amanda, not looking, gripped her bedding tighter.

Grandma began imploring Henry to eat some special Lebanese bread she had made for him, just for him. Since ancient times, throughout the Middle East, it was known to fatten up skinny people. 'Eat,' she implored, shaking the bread and coming close to Henry, who winced.

Henry's mother arrived. But Henry refused to look at her. Or speak. Suddenly he had placed a pillow over his head.

'I know you're angry,' Henry's mother said quietly to the pillow. 'Let's talk about it, Henry. Henry? Can you hear me? I've found *War and Peace*. Volume Two, unexpurgated. Henry? You were right, it was in the library stack. Henry?'

Tina hurriedly packed Peter's things. 'We must get your address,' she said to Henry's mother. 'Peter loves Henry.'

'What a good idea. Did you hear that Henry? They want our address.'

'I live at the children's hospital!' Henry shouted, briefly removing the pillow, then clamping it down again.

'Oh dear. He's never done this before. Or not for a long time–'

'Just go away!' shouted a muffled Henry.

'I'm so sorry, so rude.'

'It doesn't matter.'

The mother was weeping now.

'Je-sus, why don't you just go?' drawled Amanda, shaking her head. She pointed the remote at Peter, and pressed 'off'.

In the car park Tina's husband stood leaning against the car bonnet. 'Told you he'd be out in no time, honey,' he smiled. Tina found she was unable to smile back. His mobile rang. She buckled Peter safely into the child's seat, then, straightening, looked up towards a second-storey window, where she imagined Henry looking down at her. And she did see a shadow, behind a double-glazed window.

Uncle Dan's War

Uncle Dan was on the other side of the world, giving stick to General Rommel and his army. Dan began writing to me from the front line. He wrote every three or four weeks, between digging fox holes, crawling under barbed wire, lobbing grenades. The letters were hastily scrawled, sometimes simply a line on a postcard. They often arrived out of chronological order. I soon discovered I was the family's most reliable source of information about Dan.

I've got over the malaria, so now I'm back with my mates, I remember reading to my mother.

'I didn't even know he had malaria. That Dan!'

And another time: *Greetings, Robbie. Jerusalem's a fine city—*

'Jerusalem! So *that's* where he is.'

The women are so much friendlier here than——

'Give me that,' said my mother, snatching the letter. 'That Dan!'

Dan's tone was customarily jaunty. Sometimes it flattened. *Saw a lot of Gerry last night,* read one ominously spotted postcard, *we paid him an unexpected visit and he gave us a pretty warm welcome. Happy to report am still in one piece. Ears ringing like blasted bells. Lost a mate.*

Strings of pretty girls called by our house in that first year or two. Just passing by, they trilled – and when might Dan be home?

'That Dan!'

Sometimes parts of Dan's letters had been blacked out. 'Censored,' muttered my father, shaking his head; he had been in the last war.

I always answered Dan's letters immediately. Dan had been my favourite relative even before the war. As the war went on, my uncle increasingly confided in me, although I was only a boy. His letters became longer and more personal. In turn, mine always doubled, trebled any increase on his part. One day I received a letter that tightened my chest: *We've been chosen to go on a special mission, Robbie. Last night I had a bad dream, little mate. The dream's given me a strange feeling all day. Can't shake it. Difficult to explain. Snaky feeling. Ever been watched by a snake? Ever realised you just stepped over one? I don't know if I'm going to make it through this time. Thanks for all your letters, Robbie. You've been a real rock. Here's me moping. I'll be home in no time, no doubt, and this [censored] war will be over. P.S. Pearl hasn't dropped by, has she?*

I kept this letter under my pillow. I think the telegram arrived the next day. I remember the moment the postman handed it to my mother. No-one even knows what a telegram is anymore, but in those days they were like God's communiqués. They struck people down, lifted them up, altered them forever – all by a few staccato words. The telegram passed between the postman and my mother. Behind their almost meeting hands the hydrangea heads trembled, and I felt a fragment of the outside world lodge in our sunny doorway.

Uncle Dan had been injured in action. My mother had time to exclaim what she would – 'That Dan!' – before she collapsed, as if *she* had been injured in action. She dropped the teapot, which bounced off her shoe into the hydrangeas.

On patrol in the North African desert, Dan's unit had been ambushed by a machine-gun post. He had been shot in the head. His sixteen comrades had been killed. The enemy had walked about bayoneting anyone who moaned or moved. Only Dan had been overlooked, as he must have appeared *good as dead, Robbie. Certainly felt it. Lost a lot of mates. Thank God I wasn't taken prisoner. That's something I could not bear. I can take being shot in the head, but not being taken prisoner.* Dan had stayed face-up in the desert sun, until found by a shepherd. *They're sending me back home to get well again. P.S. Still no news of Pearl? If you happen to see her, tell her I'm coming back to be put together again, and that I'll be a better man for it.*

As soon as we were told where Dan was recuperating, my mother and I travelled to visit him. He lay on a deep verandah, first in a long line of wounded, most of them in bandages. I had a fleeting impression of viewing an exhibit -ion of mummies shipped in from Egypt. 'Here's our Dan,' said a nurse. She smiled at a man lying with a bandage about his head. We took some moments to recognise him. His exposure to the sun had marked him most. His nose had turned parti-coloured – white, purple and pink. He appeared humorous as ever. I remember him making the one-armed man in the next bed chuckle and briefly emerge from an odd dreaminess. But Dan's sentences ran down in a way that seemed new. As he trailed into silence again, I saw my mother's face briefly occupied by concern, before she remembered to hide it.

'Here's my faithful war correspondent,' Dan said, reaching out to ruffle my hair. His hand lingered. Then he fell asleep, there and then. Not before I felt blessed, however, taken up to some higher plane.

Dan was keen to get back to the front. His mates needed him, or at least his remaining mates, his new mates. 'They can't send him back,' muttered my father, 'he's already been on the front line for ten, twelve months. Longer. That's too much to ask a man, any man. No man's nerves can survive that. No man's. People simply cannot imagine...'

The war had come closer by the time Dan was deemed 'fit to resume duty'. He continued to write from the new theatre. One letter from New Guinea described a week-long sojourn inside a hollow log, where Dan had stashed himself, only for the enemy to set up camp around him, *talking in their wretched lingo*. His new best mate was in the log alongside him, but dead. *A week in the jungle is a long time to face a [censored] corpse.*

Then Dan went missing. *Missing in action*, read the telegram, and smote us.

Throughout the last years of the war, and perhaps nine or ten months after, no-one knew what had become of Dan. During that time a letter did arrive; but after our initial elation, we realised it had been sent months before his disappearance. Then, one mild and blue Sydney day, a stick figure leant in our doorway. Almost bald, missing teeth, skin blotched, off balance, an Uncle Dan scarecrow grinned in. My mother dropped the teapot, and this time it smashed.

Uncle Dan had spent the last years of the war a prisoner. I calculate that he lived with us between ten and twelve weeks, at the most. To my memory, however, this is almost unbelievable. He seemed to be with us for years.

Early in his stay – it may well have been his first morning with us – I found him naked and trembling in a doorway. 'Isn't it hot!' he said, through chattering teeth. That seemed strange, as frost covered the lawn. Days, weeks passed, and Dan never went out. Not even to the shops. He showed no inclination to visit the little church on the corner, where he had once played the organ. And when girls came to call, he hid. He would vanish into a cupboard, behind a door, under a bed; before the war, he had humoured me with games of hide and seek, and now he used these places to avoid visitors, and us. Animals seemed distasteful to him. He had loved them before the war, and had talked of becoming a vet. Once a keen reader, he had taken to closing any book he found open – after first breaking its spine – as he drifted between rooms. In the middle of an action or a sentence, he would flinch and involuntarily duck; then ten, fifteen seconds later, one of us would hear a train in the distance, labouring as it climbed the hill. Every night he yelled commands and hissed warnings, apparently from his dreams. Once, in the early hours of morning, I saw my father standing in his nightshirt outside Dan's door. Behind the door Dan could be heard loudly weeping. My father was frowning at the floor and shaking his head, muttering, 'It's not right, it's not just!'

Some mornings, Dan would be discovered in the hydrangeas. He spent whole nights in the garden, winter nights. The cover of the hydrangeas, I realised, was a place where he could view the world while remaining hidden (I had discovered this too, as a young child). And when on the verandah, Dan always sat in the shadows on the side of the house, facing out. I realised this position ensured a clear line of sight to the road. It meant sitting away from the rest of us, but to Dan a line of sight had become much more important than conversation or company. These things were to be avoided anyway, as they produced noise that might disguise other sounds. Music had become very dangerous.

Dan was particularly perturbed by the sighs and scrapes of the bamboo thicket at the bottom of the garden, and he cursed that plant almost hourly. One day he cut the lot down, completely exposing two neighbouring backyards. My mother swallowed her fury: *that Dan.*

But that Dan, each of us was silently realising, had gone. I knew it from the first day I found him, mottled and naked, squatting under the hydrangeas – I only noticed him out of the corner of my eye, after I almost passed the bush; a garden gnome, I initially thought, with a bug on it. Watching as a praying mantis did push-ups on his still and staring face, I knew *that* Dan had disintegrated in a log in New Guinea, or had been cremated, face-up, in the African sun.

My father had been trying to find Dan a job, any job, but as Dan would not leave the house, he was more or less unemployable. On each occasion that my uncle thwarted some plan for his employment, my father betrayed no anger, no frustration. And the women of the family never let up fussing over him, even as I saw them turn away, frowning and wringing their hands. My mother was especially devoted, cooking Dan a steady stream of roast dinners, broths, biscuits, cakes.

'How I hate them cooking me little cakes,' I heard Dan say one day, as he picked up and let drop one of my mother's specialities. 'Why cakes? I don't remember ever liking cakes. Did I?' He had begun drinking rather a lot, but I won't go into that.

One good thing was that Dan's hair had begun to thicken and grow lustrous again, *almost as before the war*. We all noticed it and talked about it. Every week he looked about a year younger, we reckoned. The physical Dan, at least, appeared to be on the mend, although he still trembled. After being escorted to the dentist a few times, he returned sporting a fresh set of teeth. (He had lost most of his teeth after starving in the camp.) To my mind his mouth had again altered for the worse. Everyone else, however, remarked on the improvement.

One day the most persistent of Dan's pre-war girlfriends succeeded in surprising him while he sat at the piano – not playing it, but scanning a musical score. Having read a page, Dan would tear out the page, ball it up and throw it on the ground. From being so absorbed, he twisted up with a rapid, snaking movement.

How distant and sarcastic were his replies to the young woman, Sara, as he stood by the piano not looking at her, not once, but watching his fingers drift over the keys, or kicking his shoes at the paper balls. Sara's chest rose, her chin fell, her creamy skin grew patchily pink.

I retreated to make them tea, aware of my uncle's offensively pitched voice over the noise of the kettle. The kettle began whistling. 'Turn that damned thing off!' bellowed Dan from the other room. 'I told you I can't stand it whistling! If it does that again, I'm breaking it.'

I brought them the tea. Sara had visited us the first Sunday of every month, without fail, every year Dan had been away. Perched in a pretty dress, wringing her hands in a handkerchief, Sara was the most captivating person I had ever seen.

'The one girl who hasn't been to see me is Pearl,' I heard Dan saying, not to Sara, but to the keys. 'No doubt you've heard what happened to her.'

Sara lowered her head.

'Married an American serviceman. You did know that?'

Sara nodded.

'When did she do that?' asked Dan.

'I – I can't recall,' Sara stammered.

'Was it after the war?'

'Some time after, I think.'

'Either way, I was probably still in the camp. Nice.'

Sara left with her face in her handkerchief.

Dan packed his army-issue bag after that – it might have been that afternoon – and left without saying goodbye. He caught the train north. At least that was what we supposed. Some neighbours said they had seen him standing at the station by the north-bound line. Gone to cut cane, probably, or gone jackarooing – no-one was sure. Years passed, and we never heard from him.

We never heard. I studied, launched a career in law, married and began a family. I eventually learnt, from a friend of a colleague, that Dan was living with a wife on a farm in the north of the state. I found an address, and sent a Christmas card to it every year. Dan never replied. Perhaps it was because I had married Sara.

I have reached that age at which I think back on the other men in my family, and compare their lives to mine. I have always taken an interest in character, it helps in the law. Two men in my family went to war – my father, and Dan. The quality of their war experiences is undoubtedly beyond the imagination of anyone who has not been to war. It sets them apart, and I can only surmise it must be very isolating for them. They undergo a strangely, almost peculiarly, masculine experience – that is, to be sanctioned by their society to hunt down and kill other people, usually other young men they do not know. Can you imagine getting ready to kill someone you do not know? This experience must isolate the men and boys who have gone through it – and isolate them particularly from other men. The majority of us, who have not been required to hunt and kill, must seem only partly formed to those chosen to serve. We must seem the blessedly soft, the happily ignorant ones – ignorant of *what really goes on; how things really work; what everything* (society? law? culture?) *actually rests upon.*

One day I found myself travelling on business in the state's north. I grew tempted to visit Dan. I had recently reread his wartime correspondence, about a dozen surviving letters and postcards preserved in a rusty biscuit tin. Surely Dan would want to see me? I was now fifty, worldly (or what passed as worldly), inevitably hardened: yet still inside me was an invulnerable vulnerable core, if I could put it that way. That is, I still yearned to see the people I had loved. That never changed, no matter what. Surely it is the same with everyone, and the same with Dan. What could extinguish that core? People never change, in essence – do they?

Driving to a client's home, I realised I was not far from Dan's property. After attending to the day's business, I booked a room in the only pub in a small, rather sterile-looking town. Settling at the bar that night, I asked after my uncle.

'Dan, eh? From the big smoke originally, you say? Married May? Haven't seen him in yonks, you say?' The bartender was not only repeating everything I said, he was repeating it loudly. People in the pub began to turn their heads. The bartender's towelled fist turned inside a schooner glass. 'Reckon you're related to our local hermit, eh? He locks up May, you know.'

'Pardon?'

'I said he locks up your aunt.'

'I don't know about that.'

'Well, I'm telling you,' said the bartender. 'They used to come into town, him and May. Now they get everything delivered. Lots of people ask after her. But you're the first to ask after *him*.'

The bartender eyed me steadily, and hung the glass. A white-haired woman stood up from a group drinking in a corner. She approached me. 'I couldn't help overhearing,' she said. 'Your uncle married my best friend.'

'Glad to meet you,' I said.

She ignored my extended hand.

'May was our town's most vivacious girl,' the woman informed me, 'and the prettiest. Then she married that man. Is he really your uncle?'

Thanks for all your letters, Robbie. You've been a real rock.

'Look, I haven't seen my uncle Dan in over thirty years, not since I was a kid—'

'Then I'll tell it to you straight. Your uncle destroyed our May. He came up from the city, not caring less.' *That Dan.* 'He sweet-talked May and married her. Then he locked her up. Oh, it happened bit by bit, over the years, but now we never see her. Why? Can you answer me that?'

'Look, lady, let's establish some facts—'

'Don't "lady" me. If I could tell you how fine she was … and now she's a prisoner in her own home.'

'First, what evidence—'

'I can't visit. He got rid of me. He got rid of all her friends, one by one. There's no phone in the place. The gate's padlocked. As God is my witness, she could be dead for all we know. That's what your uncle's done. He's taken a life.'

'Look, Uncle Dan went through hell, absolute hell, that's beyond question. I suppose you are aware he was a POW?'

'Then I wish they had never let him out.'

The woman walked away, patting her hair. Her farmer friends glared from their corner. Two women stroked their country sister.

'Welcome to town!' the barman grinned, and winked. 'She must have taken a bit of a shine to Dan herself, eh? Even I remember those perfect teeth. Same again?'

The next morning I drove past a series of orchards, checking the numbers on the occasional letterboxes. I think I am fairly thick-skinned these days, but I admit I had replayed that conversation in the bar more than a few times in my head – I had to keep telling myself to stop thinking about it. I came to a property where the grass was growing over the fence. The gate was padlocked. After a moment's consideration, I climbed over. The long driveway was weedy. High kikuyu grew into an orchard, where patches of torn netting hung from the trees. A flat-tired tractor stood in a rusty shed. I passed a line of hydrangeas, and hesitated, almost turned back. But I could see the house, and knew, by the stiffening of hairs on my skin, that I was being observed.

The house, surrounded by rose-beds, stood on a slight rise.

I knocked, then knocked again. I tapped on a window. Curtains parted.

'Yes? What do you want?' A voice interrogated me through the glass.

'Uncle Dan?'

'Who are you?'

'It's me.'

'Who might *me* be?'

'It's me, Robbie.'

'Who is Robbie?'

'Your nephew.'

The curtains closed. I waited. At last I heard a series of locks opening behind the door, from the top almost to the floor. The door opened a little, and Uncle Dan peered through the crack. For a moment I thought I was looking at the wrong man. His neck and face were blotched, blemishes I only now remembered. He seemed twenty or thirty years older than me, although our age difference was only eight or nine years.

'I – I was in this neck of the woods–'

Dan's head jerked towards the interior of the house, and he opened the door.

I thought he was going to ruffle my hair as I passed. Instead he indicated one of several chairs. I sat as directed, facing Dan.

Dust sheets covered every piece of furniture. In the near-silence, only the brier-roses moved, wavering at the window panes. Perhaps it is the roses that made the tapping, so faint, and rather irregular.

'Why have you come?'

'Why – to see you – and Aunt May.' I found myself blushing, for the first time in decades.

'You mean Pearl?'

'No … May.'

'I'm married to Pearl. I call her Pearl.'

'Pearl, then.'

'Oh, Pearl's a bit ill, I'm afraid. She's become increasingly frail lately. I'm looking after her. We don't often have visitors. We don't get out much.'

'How are *you*, Uncle Dan?'

'Me? I'm getting on a bit, Robbie. My war wounds are catching up with me. I still can't sleep.'

He seemed to coil down into himself. Then he rose up out the chair, and limped off to make tea.

The little roses wavered at the window. Old-fashioned, scented roses. Planted by a woman.

Sipping from our matching cups, I found myself listening closely to spaces, to silences, calculating the dimensions of rooms in the place.

'Is she in bed?' I asked.

Dan dipped his biscuit in his tea, looked at the carpet, and did not answer.

'It must be hard looking after the farm and – and Pearl.'

'I don't go in for farming any longer, Robbie. I've got my war pension.'

'Do you need any help?'

He looked up quickly. 'Oh no. You can't trust anyone around here.' Dan smoothed the sheet on an adjacent sofa. 'A town full of snakes.'

Soon I was hurriedly retreating to the road. My uncle's gaze followed me down to the gate. I turned for a last look, almost defiantly. In an upstairs window, a curtain had been pulled aside. Something dark crossed the glass, and I distinctly heard the window click shut.

'So you didn't end up finding the lost uncle, eh?' asked the bartender, polishing the last of the glasses. I had been sitting alone at the bar, watching him finish up for the night.

'N-n-no,' I answered, and heard my speech slur. 'No. I told you I didn't find him. Another, thanks. Same again.'

'You don't want a glass of water instead?'

'What? No.'

'Well – you know best. Case of mistaken identity, was it?'

'Hey?'

'With the bloke you thought was your uncle?'

'Absolutely. Turned out to be someone I never knew. Some old guy messed up in the head by the war. Tragedy. What a tragedy. That's war, eh? Destroys … destroys *relationships*.'

'You can say that again,' said the barman.

'Eh?'

'I said you can say that again!'

'Yes, same again.'

Vivien's Fingers

Do we have to take it?' asked Dean.

'It was bequeathed to us.'

'I can't play the piano. Neither can you.'

'My grandmother wanted me to have it.'

It was not true that Vivien could not play. She had not played for many years. Certainly not since she married Dean.

The piano had ended up in the 'study', an empty little room at the back of the house looking onto the garden.

She did not touch the piano for weeks. Then, one morning, while the baby slept, she placed a hand on the keys, experiencing their ivory coolness for the first time since girlhood. The keys dipped in the shape of fingers, her grandmother's fingers. Vivien's hand of itself formed an E minor chord – the blue chord, she remembered. Why hadn't she struck out on sunny C major?

The baby began to cry, and she closed the lid.

'Remember you asked me what I wanted for my birthday?' Vivien asked Dean when he got home from work that night. She was between feeding the baby and bathing the baby.

'Yes, honey?'

'I'd like some piano lessons.'

He said nothing. A few nights later, when she mentioned it again, he said, 'But that's money down the drain, isn't it?'

'I want to learn again. That's not money down the drain, is it? It's a birthday present, Dean.'

He agreed, although it meant he would have to look after the baby whenever she had a lesson. He had been working long hours, and had spent little time with Erica.

Vivien arrived early for her first lesson. The teacher was an old friend, Jill, who held the lessons in her rather grandmotherly living room. Vivien had been there many times before, yet she waited anxiously on the edge of a chair, her palms tacky. Jill was instructing a small boy, who broke off playing *Greensleeves* to stare at Vivien.

'Is *she* next?' he asked.

'Yes, Bradley, she's learning piano too,' said Jill. 'Now, where were we?'

'But she's old.'

Bradley was persuaded to resume, although it might as well have been *Greensleeves* backwards.

'G *natural*, Bradley,' coaxed Jill, 'not G sharp. And remember, these are not crotchets. What do we call them again?'

Later in the week, Dean leafed through Vivien's piano book, *Let's Have Fun! Piano One*. 'You're playing children's pieces,' he remarked.

'I have to start somewhere.'

'It's a bit late, isn't it?' asked Dean.

'Late for what?'

'Don't be so defensive.' He closed the book, and put it down on the wet kitchen bench.

'You've hardly been encouraging, Dean.'

'I've paid for the term's lessons, haven't I?'

'Has Erica been crying like that all morning?' asked Vivien.

'She doesn't like me looking after her. She only wants you.'

'Rubbish. Has she eaten anything this morning?'

'I have tried, Vivien; I tell you, she doesn't want me looking after her – she wants you, not me. She won't let me feed her.'

'Don't be ridiculous,' said Vivien.

At first Vivien made little or no progress. She marvelled at Bradley's *Greensleeves*. And she marvelled at her lost ability. Her fingers, which she had always thought agile, proved leaden.

They would not budge at her brain's commands. Of course it did not help that she was only able to find five minutes to practise here, ten minutes there, before the baby began screaming. Vivien swore that Erica could detect the instant she sat at the piano. The child had an extra sense – the same sense that made her cry the moment Vivien finally sat down to eat, or the moment Vivien and Dean started to have sex – not that that happened often these days.

Sometimes Vivien played straight through Erica's worst howls. Thinking back, she would discover a run of ellipses running through the music, like a run in a mental stocking.

Jill, satisfied that Vivien had reacquired *Greensleeves* and *Twinkle Twinkle Little Star*, issued Vivien with *See What You Can Do! Piano Two*.

Vivien found she was more exhausted than usual, more crotchety. She thought it was from doggedly reabsorbing the symbols encoding the music – the legers, staves, clefs and slurs. Or not so much reabsorbing as exhuming them. She was learning again a language half-grasped in childhood. It was also the language understood across centuries and continents, and she liked to imagine those who had shared it, people who had read the same symbols she now deciphered – perhaps some child in, say, Mexico, two centuries ago … or a smooth-faced girl in Japan, during the war … or a dreamy-eyed Russian at the time of Prokofiev and the Revolution … Dean always shut the study door when she practised.

'The piano's out of tune,' Vivien told Dean at the end of the first term's lessons. 'I'm going to call a piano tuner.'

'How much will that cost?' he asked. 'Can't you put up with it for the time being?'

'Every time I hit certain notes I wince.'

'I can't hear it.'

She asked him again a week later.

'No, we can't afford a piano tuner,' he replied, 'that's not in the budget. Maybe it's the way you're playing that makes it sound bad.'

Vivien began saving for the piano tuner. It was important. The music was coming back, and she wanted it cared for, welcomed and never again abandoned.

Her new piano book might be titled *Music Is Easy! Piano Three*, but she found music returned through dull headaches. The part of the brain that received messages and transmitted them to her fingers actually ached, physically hurt. She had read somewhere that the bundle of neurones in a musician's brain administering fingers (or, in some cases, lips) grows. Well, it sure felt like it. She could almost see the nerves bulging from her cortex to her wrist. Yet sometimes, in the middle of a phrase, or after correctly completing a scale, the neural pathway tingled nicely, like sensation returning into an old burn. She was retracing childhood pathways.

Meanwhile, Erica was always screaming because she could not quite crawl. Vivien and the child became locked in a contest: Erica to crawl, Vivien to consolidate at least some musical proficiency.

One day Vivien became aware of a knocking at the front door, just audible above her playing and the baby's screams. She knew the knock, and sighed. At this time, few things exasperated Vivien more than being interrupted by Penny, her near neighbour. Penny insisted on dropping in once or twice a week, usually just as Vivien had found a minute to sit at the piano; Vivien would close her piano book, fold away her resentment, and make the good woman tea.

'I hear you playing the piano rather a lot,' Penny put in at some point in every conversation. 'I'm not sure how you find the time.'

'Erica's a good sleeper.'

'I thought you said—'

'She's become one. I think the piano helps her sleep.'

One drizzling, red-leafed autumn morning, Penny asked if it was hard, playing the piano? Vivien was looking out the kitchen window, rinsing the teapot, visualising the awkward fingering of the B-flat scale. She needed it for *Mozart And More! Piano Four.*

'As hard as you want it to be,' answered Vivien.

'Goodness. That does sound hard.'

'It's endless. I can't imagine anyone ever completely mastering the piano.'

'Then why do you bother?'

It was a good question from Penny. 'I think it's because all the women in my family played the piano.' All the women – Vivien had not realised that until she said it. They had revered the piano, excelled at it; her grandmother had been a concert pianist.

Vivien glanced at the kitchen clock, speculating when Penny might leave, and when Erica would wake, and calculating the interval.

Vivien had known most of the pieces as a child, and they came back up out of the grain. With each piece she gained a vista of girlhood: a pond of lilies by the swing in her grandmother's garden, encrypted in Grieg; in Scarlatti, bars of sunlight slanting over an open chest of toys; Mozart meant her mother and grandmother playing at the one piano, bobbing and laughing. Then Vivien would feel how time had passed, and panic – she had wasted so much time, and so little time was left, and babies ate time. As did marriages.

Sometimes there was no struggle. Sometimes her fingers agreed to whatever she asked of them. They opened the door a little more, that door first prised ajar in childhood, and she peered onto the original world again. Birds came to the window then, blue-breasted, pirouetting, trilling. In those moments she remembered stretching on the carpet as a small child, listening to notes showering down from the sky, as if down bright glistening staircases in the ether. The notes, produced by her grand-mother and mother, seemed curiously scarlet, as the women swooped through an arrangement for two pianos of Handel's The Arrival of the Queen of Sheba. The music fell in such profusion, and with such fluidity that it was difficult for a child to place the roof back on the house, let alone close heaven. From then on, there remained the possibility of a passage from the inner life to heaven.

When she practised, Dean liked to whistle tuneless ditties, attempts at pop tunes. He would interrupt to ask about the baby: Sorry, honey, but what bottle had been sterilised? That one – or this? Could you look? You said this one, but would you mind stopping a moment and checking? Was this the right temperature for the milk? How could you tell without feeling it? Darling, when did Erica last sleep?

He might say something else that she would not hear. She was learning that. The music gave her a place from which to ignore him. She was strong there, and he would walk away muttering, holding the baby. He was spending more and more time with Erica.

Vivien took to lying Erica on a couch beside the piano, where she could watch her daughter from the corner of her eye as she played. Vivien would race to perfect some phrase as Erica dragged herself towards the couch's edge.

One day Erica fell. The child began fitting; her little back arched, her eyes rolled, her limbs stiffened. Her face and fingers turned an eggshell blue, speckled red.

A few hours later, the doctor was reassuring Vivien and Dean that no permanent damage had been done; look, Erica was sitting up on the examining table – although she was still grizzling, rejecting the surgery's toys, and she would not be cuddled by Vivien, she only wanted Dean.

'Did you see Erica roll off the couch, Vivien?' asked the doctor.

'Well, no.'

'Where were you?' asked Dean, who had rushed to the surgery from work.

Vivien did not answer.

The doctor said quickly, 'Let me repeat, no damage has been done. But let's try to get to the bottom of this. The fall might have caused the fit, or Erica might have fallen due to the fit. I think the latter. Had you noticed she does have a temperature? That she does have an infection?'

'I hadn't noticed,' said Vivien.

'How could you not notice?' cried Dean.

Later he said to her, 'You don't care if she's crying. You just keep playing that piano. You could have killed her.'

'It doesn't do her any harm to let her cry awhile. They say twenty minutes.'

'No, no, let her cry, let her have her seizure.'

'The doctor said the febrile convulsion was most likely a one-off,' said Vivien, 'that little children sometimes have them at Erica's age when they have a fast-rising temperature. She's not neglected, Dean.'

'You're not focused on her; you're focussed on the piano. Erica picks up on that, you know. All the damage is done in the first few years.'

Vivien turned away, reading but not reading *Jumpin' Jive! Piano Five*.

She had asked her mother to pay for the next term's lessons.

According to Jill, Vivien had begun to make real progress. Yes, the music was flowing back. Vivien pictured the return as ganglions of nerves knitting together, forking through scar tissue. *Jumpin' Jive! Piano Five*, however, presented many challenges, and one morning Dean found Vivien weeping, despairing that she could not play something; she was wrestling with a difficult time signature, and losing. It was too hard.

'Why do you persist, Vivien? You've been playing that same phrase or whatever over and over the entire morning, driving us both insane. You haven't even heard Erica crying, have you?'

'What? No. What's wrong with her?'

'You didn't hear because the piano's too loud?'

'Of course not! That baby can be heard a mile away!'

Erica, who could now crawl, poked her head about the door. She looked at Vivien, who sat hunched at the piano stool. Then she looked up at her father.

'Look, Vivien, why can't you try to get a balance—'

'It doesn't sound any good unless you play a certain amount, Dean. Unless you practise a lot it sounds terrible. I'm either committed or I don't do it at all, there's no point. I never get a chance to practise enough, that's why it's not sounding any good, that's why I'm so frustrated and angry all the time. I have glimpses of where I'm meant to be going, but not the time or energy to get there. The only time I feel happy is when I play the piano. It's the only thing I have left for myself. I'm sorry the music sounds so bad–'

'I don't care what it sounds like, Vivien—'

'No! And that's the pity!'

'I can't win with you,' Dean snarled. He glared at the piano. Suddenly he bared his teeth, craned forward, and slammed down the lid.

'That almost caught my fingers, Dean!'

'Damn your fingers.'

Dean wheeled about, and nearly tripped over Erica, who took several seconds to comprehend things were not good, no, they were bad. And it was the piano that was the problem, the piano.

Soon Erica learnt to walk. She liked to stand by the piano, following Vivien's fingers. One day the child slammed down the lid.

Erica scurried under her bed.

'I said come out from under there, you little –!' cried Vivien, her fingers in a bowl of ice. Soon she changed her tactics. 'It's alright, darling, Mummy won't hurt you, come and get a chocolate. Can you have two? Yes, you can even have two. Mummy got a shock, that's all, but she's not mad now.'

'Mummy is hurt.'

'Nothing's broken, darling. Mummy's fingers are a little bit bruised, that's all. But it was all Mummy's fault.'

At last Erica, covered in dust, emerged from under the bed, and Vivien gave her a one-armed hug. 'I think you might have become a little Daddy's girl, haven't you?' she said. Then she took the child to the piano, and showed her what it felt like to place fingers on the keys.

The next morning Vivien surrendered her music books to Jill. It was not so much the slamming of the piano lid that had decided her; it was the recollection of a dust- and cobweb-covered Erica appearing from under the bed.

'Maybe you'll pursue the piano again later in life,' said Jill, taking the books reluctantly.

'Of course I will,' said Vivien, recalling the final snap of the piano lid, the last jazzy chord extemporised under her splayed fingers.

'I do think you're very talented, Vivien. You really need a new teacher, someone to take you to the next level.'

After that Vivien's life became much simpler, really only a matter of how to get through the day.

One morning, Penny was demonstrating to Vivien the best way to make a teacake. Penny lifted the finished product from the oven, and slid the cake with a thud onto the kitchen table. 'There!' she sighed, righting the cake and placing it on a rack, 'we've done it, and it's just *perfect*. But I never hear you play the piano any more, Vivien,' she frowned, as she poured melted butter over the golden cake. 'You really have given it up, haven't you?'

Vivien could hear the clock ticking, but did not look.

'It was too hard, Penny.'

'Well, I think it's a great pity,' said Penny, who made a curious clucking sound. 'It was starting to sound really good. I mean it. Is Erica going to learn the piano? If it runs in the family—'

'Erica may learn in time.'

Penny sprinkled a mixture of cinnamon and sugar on the shining dome of the cake-top. She sighed again. Yes, the cake was just perfect, and they should start eating it immediately.

Erica darted into the kitchen to snatch a slice of the cake, before running back down the hall. Penny and Vivien listened to Erica banging away randomly at the piano – all that cinnamon, butter and ivory. The piano was Erica's favourite plaything at the moment; she even liked to stand on it.

The Glider

When I was a child I defaced a rock painting. It was years ago, I was only ten or eleven – I'm forty now. But lately I've been thinking about it a lot. In fact, I've thought about it ever since, on and off. It's one of those things that have continued to worry me, a memory that rather than fades only grows with time. A regret.

Another kid showed me the painting. He was my next-door neighbour. We were wagging school and hanging out in the bush. We used to lie about on slabs of rock, talking about stuff, while looking up through the gum trees. One day he announced he'd found a cave with a painting in it. Did I want to go and see? Of course I did. The cave wasn't hard to get to. We just crossed over the little gully in the bush behind my place, climbed the rocks, and there it was, a rock ledge with a cave at the back with a big painting. I couldn't believe it had been there all the time, right behind where I lived. From the cave I could even see, through the trees, the roof of my house.

'The blacks did the painting,' Mick had said – that was my friend's name.

'What, do blacks live around here?' I remember asking. I knew it was a stupid question, but the painting really surprised me, and in one way it didn't look that old.

'Nah, they're gone now. Ages ago.'

'How long gone?' I asked.

I remember feeling a bit scared. The cicadas suddenly fell simultaneously silent, the way they do. That still spooks me.

It wasn't my idea to deface the painting. Mick suggested it. He was my only friend at the time and I suppose I wanted to impress him. So when he dared me to scratch out and draw over the painting, I did it. I hadn't got far before I was feeling sick somehow. I'd never vandalised anything before. Mick said it wasn't vandalism, the painting wasn't anybody's property, not any longer – was it? But I could tell he wasn't too happy, either. We walked home in silence, and that turned out to be the last time we ever went down to the bush together. We stopped being friends after that. We suddenly became embarrassed or ashamed of one another, and he called me stuck-up because my mum was a doctor. I'd lost my friend.

The rock painting showed a feather-tail glider. I recall that clearly. I recognised the representation straight away, because we had gliders about our house. Gliders inhabited our suburb – still do, in fact. I've always liked them, and feel some sort of affinity with them. Compared to your average possum they're small, very light, with bright detailed faces, large night eyes, a glossy dark streak along their 'wings' and beautiful feathery tails. They can glide a surprisingly long way, and not necessarily in a straight line. Once I saw one swerve around the television aerial of our house.

As I've said, I've often thought about the painting – usually when I'm depressed, I don't know why. The defacing marks some low point in my emotional life. I was an unpopular kid, unhappy and lonely, with no father. Nowadays I always know when I'm stressed, because I dream about the glider, and it intrudes upon my daytime thoughts. And another thing: it seems gliders appear at important moments in my life – auspicious and inauspicious. I saw one the night before my last big university exams. One appeared the evening I broke up with my only serious girlfriend. And I saw a glider the morning my mother died; I'd never seen one in the morning before.

Being a vet I quite often have gliders brought into work. Cats delight to catch, yet hesitate to eat them. I spend a lot of time and money caring for them, to be honest. And I've made it my business to learn as much as I can about gliders. I don't want to boast, but it seems I have a kind of talent for them (other people have remarked upon it). Sometimes vets discover a talent for treating certain animals, a sympathy for a line of species. There's some kind of affinity there. The local zoo has asked me to work with its native animals, and I'm happy to do this in my spare time.

I've often wondered who did that painting of the glider. Lately I've been researching the local Indigenous people. But I've found little information about them or their beliefs, although they alone lived here until so recently, when you think about it – my short life span only four or five times over. Some of what I have learnt intrigues me. Just little things. For example, they were reported to have been unusually tall, averaging over six feet. That must have been striking, especially to Europeans in the eighteenth century. They were apparently monotheistic. A local community does still exist, something I only discovered recently. They keep a low profile, however.

The funny thing is I saw my old friend Mick the other night, for the first time in close to thirty years. I went down to the local pub after work, something I rarely do. I was upset, I'd just put down a dog and the owner was distraught and blamed me for not saving the animal. (That's the worst part of my job – having to tell people their pets are going to die. They don't prepare you for that at vet school. Every day I'm amazed at how important animals are to people. Every day I have pet-owners weeping in my surgery.) Anyway, having to break bad news has been getting to me recently – I feel it's getting harder, not easier. So I went to the pub to settle down before going home. There was Mick. I recognised him immediately. He told me he drives heavy equipment for the local council. Almost straightaway we began talking about the painting of the feather-tail glider – and it turns out that thing we did has been bugging him too, all these years.

It was actually good to talk to Mick again. I felt something had been put to rest. We ended up having more than a few beers. I felt shocking the next morning at work, and almost lost a cat.

As we were saying goodbye, I suggested we meet this Sunday morning, and go back to look at the painting. It was a spur of the moment suggestion, I don't know what made me say it, and he seemed surprised. But he agreed. Whether he'll turn up or not, I don't know.

'How many have you had?' asked Donna.

'Hey? Only a couple.'

'Mick—'

'Well, it was hot today,' said Mick. 'Bloody hard work – bulldozing down trees and yanking out bloody roots.'

'But you knocked off four hours ago,' observed Donna. She was washing up.

'Kids still up?' asked Mick.

'Why not? It's not too late.'

'There, you said it yourself – it's not too late.'

Mick and Donna's three children could be seen in the adjacent room, perched before the television.

'Give me a kiss,' mumbled Mick.

'You're pissed,' said Donna.

'Only a little. But I've got a bloody good excuse. I met this bloke in the pub–'

'Oh great. So we've got another flat-screen TV—'

'No, no, no, it's not like that,' said Mick. 'We were kids together. Hadn't seen him in thirty bloody years. And there he was, sitting there in the exact same place I usually sit. He recognised me straight off. *You're Mick*, he said. He was a bit stuck-up when he was a kid. His mum was a doctor. But he seemed happy enough to see me.'

'Fascinating. The people you meet in the pub.'

Donna put on the kettle, a sign of disapproval.

'He told me a story,' said Mick. 'So I had to listen, didn't I?'

'Depends what kind of story.'

'Hey kids, want to hear a story?' shouted Mick.

The children, still before the screen, did not stir.

'This bloke's name is Dennis. He's turned out alright, he's actually the local vet. We used to get in trouble together.'

'Here we go. What kind of trouble?'

'Well, nothing bad, not really. He's a funny kind of bloke, Dennis, always was. We weren't that suited. He read books and stuff. Quiet, you know. But we kind of got on – for about a year, at least. He never had a dad – same as me, see. There was one thing we did, that's what we ended up talking about.'

The kettle began rumbling. Donna yawned. 'You sound like long-lost pals, I must say. He's not a poofter, is he?'

'No. Well, I dunno, really. He's no man's man.'

'What did you talk about?'

'Now that's the funny bit. Hey kids, want to hear a story?'

Troy, the eldest, turned his head. 'What kind of story?' he asked. It was the ads.

'A ghost story.'

'Ghost story?' Troy's head remained in profile.

'You've been drinking, Mick,' said Donna. 'You don't sound yourself.'

Troy came into the kitchen.

'Do you believe in ghosts, son?' asked Mick.

'Nah.'

'There's a boy.'

'What, so you're not going to tell the story?' asked Troy.

'Of course I am, son. When I was about your age I had this friend. We weren't best friends. But we used to go down the bush together, down the gully at the back here, and look about, you know. Like you do. Get up to things.'

'Don't put ideas in his head,' said Donna.

'And there was a cave there, on the ridge above.'

'Where?' asked Troy.

'Never you mind, son. And it had a painting. Kind of – special it was – the painting. And the place. Couldn't describe it exactly. I suppose it's still there.'

'What kind of painting, Dad?'

'A rock painting.'

'You mean by blacks?'

'Yeah.'

'You mean blacks live round here?' asked Troy excitedly.

'Yeah. I mean no. But they used to, of course they did.'

'What kind of painting was it?'

'A painting of an animal,' said Mick. 'A glider.'

'Can I go and see it?'

'What? No.'

'Why not?'

'Because being naughty little buggers, you know what we did to that painting?' The kettle began to whistle. 'We stuffed it up.'

'Why do a thing like that, Dad?'

'Donna, I might have another beer,' said Mick.

'No, you won't.'

'Love, the kid wants to hear the story. And I need a drink to keep me going. This is hard work, this telling stories.'

'Go on, let him, Mum. Dad's never told a ghost story before. So you mucked up the painting.'

'Yeah, we … we did it,' said Mick. 'Or he did it. Dennis did it. It was his idea. It was a – what do they call them? – a feather-tail glider, or so he reckons, although I don't remember that. We were sort of daring each other, egging one another on, you know, because it was kind of … *spooky* in that place.'

'You shouldn't be telling him this,' said Donna. 'You shouldn't tell anyone. You might get in trouble these days.'

'He's old enough. I want to tell someone.'

'So what's it all about?' cried Troy. 'That's not a ghost story.'

Mick suddenly looked at his blunt, stained fingers.

'You might make me a coffee, thanks love,' he said softly.

'Dad!'

'Time for bed, son.'

'That's not fair. You said it was going to be a ghost story. I stopped watching TV to come and hear this – and it's bloody stupid. It just shows you were – well, stupid.' Troy stomped off.

'Now look what you've done, Mick. I'd just got them settled and ready for bed. What's got into you?'

'Come here, love, sit here,' said Mick. 'It was a funny thing, Dennis mentioning that painting. I got bitten by a glider once. My finger went that red–'

'Vicious little things.'

'No, not at all. Haven't you seen one? They're like little flying possums. Well, they are little flying possums. Amazing, isn't it – that a possum can fly, or glide at least. This one was injured and I tried to pick it up. The cat had got it and dropped it at the door. That's when the feather-tail bit me. My finger got that infected I had trouble working for a week.'

Troy reappeared in the kitchen doorway, brushing his teeth.

'Dad, this Dennis idiot – has he fixed the painting?'

'No. He couldn't have fixed it, son. It was ruined. We made sure of that.'

Troy spat out the toothpaste in the sink, rinsing his mouth. 'That sucks.'

Mick felt silly about going to look at the painting when Sunday morning came; but he had promised, and he kept promises, even ones made at the pub. He told Donna he was going to the hardware.

The two men met at the back of Dennis's childhood home. What had once been paddocks was now a sea of houses. The steep gully and its ridge behind the houses, however, had been preserved.

'Thanks for coming, Mick,' said Dennis.

'Oh, you know. I've done the mowing. Hey, I saw a feather-tail last night. It was running along the telephone wires.'

'There are some still around.'

The men puffed their way down the rocks, sliding between trees, joking about how old and stiff they had become. They came to a rock ledge where they had once sat and talked. 'Hang on, my name's carved on this rock somewhere,' said Mick. 'Here it is! And here's your name, Denny. How about that, eh?'

The cicadas stopped singing; the men looked up together. Light revolved in the crowns of the gums.

'I'm sorry I said those things about your mum – you know – when I was a kid,' said Mick.

'What things?'

'You know, that you were stuck-up because she was a doctor. You probably don't remember.'

'Don't worry about it.'

They set off again, crossing the oily, almost unmoving stream at the bottom of the gully. 'We'll need a drink after this,' gasped Mick, as they clambered up the ridge. 'Hey, there's the cave. Looks exactly the same from here.'

Across the gully a mower coughed into life. The cicadas paused again, and the men turned towards the suburb. But the trees had grown and now hid the houses. The cicadas resumed, enclosing the men in a sheer curtain of song. Mick and Dennis lowered their heads and climbed the last few steps, each intent on his own thoughts. They had their memories, their regrets, and no inkling of what they might find.

Love

As Thomas turned the car into his street, a woman advanced in stages through the windscreen wipers. She was walking in the storm with no umbrella. He drew alongside and wound down the window. Did she want a lift?

The woman kept her head down. Thomas could barely see the houses beyond the beaten hydrangea heads.

'Excuse me! A lift?'

The woman glanced in Thomas's direction. He was stretched across the handbrake, holding open the passenger door. After a pause she appeared to recognise Thomas, and got in, bringing with her the smell of wet wool. She lived around the next corner, she told him. Thomas released the handbrake; he could still smell the wool while he concentrated on the road.

'You live in that house there,' the woman volunteered. Thomas looked, as if needing to check – and for a moment, he did not recognise his house. It seemed shrunken. The tops of surrounding trees flayed its roof, and the windows were dark and blank. 'I've seen you before,' the woman added, a raindrop hanging from the tip of her nose. 'You're a good man,' she said, as a rivulet of rain plummeted down her neck. 'You stopped for me. Here – this is where I live.'

They idled outside a little house he had never really noticed before; it was only around the corner from his home. The woman half turned her face towards him. Afterwards he realised he had gleaned a particular impression, but for the moment he was only aware of her face as broad and flat, something young over a timeless frame. Then he watched her pass through sheets of water, like a bather through a waterfall, her sagging woollen jumper gathered in folds on her hips. The front of the car felt abruptly too large and empty.

He was entirely absent when he got home, until his wife's voice parted his thoughts.

'Thomas?'

'Sorry, Miranda?'

'Beans or peas?'

'Nice meal,' he said, as the food returned him by degrees to the present. He considered telling Miranda about the woman in the rain. A little internal voice said, *No, don't*: so he did, because he wanted no secrets from his wife.

'The woman was getting wet?' asked Miranda.

'Saturated. She only lives around the corner.'

'Do we know her?'

'No,' said Thomas, 'although I think I've seen her before. She was familiar somehow.'

Miranda looked down at some work papers before her on the table.

'You're a good man,' she said, catching his hand as he passed her some moments later. Miranda often said these words to him, but it had been some time since he had really heard them, or felt them. Now he looked at Miranda, trying to take her in as he had absorbed the damp stranger.

The next morning he found the woman's umbrella in his car. So she'd had an umbrella. That was strange. He would have to take it back.

Standing before the woman's door, Thomas noticed things seemed to warp and stretch here, just here, on her path. Maybe it was the sun, appearing timidly so that the house shimmered in a rainwater film. Lilies grew by the door, water cupped in each flower's throat.

When the woman did not immediately appear at his knock, Thomas left the umbrella on the step. He had already turned to leave when the door opened, and the woman peered from the darkness. Her hair was still wet – or rather, it was wet again. She appeared in a hurry, and talked over him, and in her hurry insisted he come in. Holding only a towel about her, closing the door, she dashed down a short hall into another room. The towel slid from under her shoulder blades, revealing her back, hips and some of her behind. She was shorter than he had realised, stockier. He felt himself flush, but internally, and something solid in him melted in the heat, and drained away.

Soon she reappeared in just a slip.

'I won't stay,' said Thomas, 'I only wanted to return –'

'I made a pot of tea before I jumped in for a quick shower. It'll be ready now.'

'There's no need –'

'But I want to say thank you for helping me.'

She was already reaching for the cups.

'You left your umbrella in my car,' explained Thomas, and he held it up, thinking, *Leave the umbrella and go*, but it was as if someone he had just learnt to ignore was telling him.

'One of the bits is broken,' said the woman, taking the clammy object. 'See? It doesn't go up properly. I'm a bit of a perfectionist.' She was sure of something now, as she poured the tea. 'I don't think you've asked my name. It's Hannah.'

Rain was falling again. Drops hung on the kitchen window; the drops grew, fattened and slid under their own weight. Leaves dithered beyond the glass. Hannah's shoulders and chest were exposed as her round arms extended. Thomas did not look away. The moment was entirely sown up now, suspended outside the day. Hannah was almost matronly, yet childless – somehow he knew that. She smelt of milk, and some underlying sweetness, perhaps lilac, or lavender. The window made him think of his house around the corner – and it seemed Hannah and he might be in another century, on another continent. From an unsuspected gestation he felt the nudge and twitch of a dormant self. His thoughts flowed from their accustomed medium into another medium entirely, the way food is transformed into flesh, or the way the sugar crystals were dissolving in his tea.

'Have you lived here long?' he asked, not to know, but to listen to her. He wanted the moment to keep flowing over.

'This is my mother's house,' said Hannah. 'Or it was. I moved in to nurse her last year. She died.'

Hannah began to cry. Faint freckles emerged from under the tracks of her tears. He put his arm about her shoulders; and then he kissed the top of her head, where a jagged run exposed her scalp.

'Thank you,' she said. 'I needed that.'

'I've got to go,' he said. This time, she let him.

I should invite her to dinner, thought Thomas as he drove away, *Hannah needs a friend, she is alone and upset about her mother, so I should invite her to meet Miranda.* He clutched to these thoughts as to the flotsam of his former self. But as he parked the car, then climbed the station steps, he had already given himself up to dwelling upon her words, her movements, her flesh, the space it seemed she had always occupied inside him. He pictured a space left inside him at birth, like a pocket of air trapped inside a cast, which she filled.

The train came. He sat in the old carriage, looking out the same window people had gazed through over decades. He saw the shell of a new building rising over a bend in the line, and he almost came to for a moment. Then the train plunged into a tunnel, and his mind dwelt upon Hannah with a raw, abounding energy he had forgotten he possessed. The train was under the city now, and he craved for the darkness of the tunnel to continue. His station came, slowly, with green tiles.

Then he was on an escalator climbing towards the sun, returning guardedly to his former self. *What's going on, Thomas? Why linger in that woman's house – and why did you kiss her hair?* He never flirted, he left no feelers out. He was a married man, taking it for granted any woman other than his wife would essentially ignore him, and he her, other than to be cordial. He and Miranda were happy together – weren't they? They had been.

So why did he think of Hannah all day? Imagining meeting her again, or revisiting what he had glimpsed of her body? Had he always had this chink in his self? How could such a chink remain hidden so long?

The day passed in a dream-like interval: it took so long to pass so quickly. When he alighted at his stop after work, the unchanged station made him realise how altered he was. Since the morning, every moment with Hannah had grown and bloomed with repeated rehearsal.

'Hello,' her voice piped from the shadows. 'We must have been on the same train.'

They contemplated this.

'Do you want a lift?' he asked after some moments. 'The rain's returning.'

So they sat beside one another again, while the rain swam the windscreen, and the first rainy drive became fixed and set by the second rainy drive. It passed so smoothly, so inevitably, he could not feel his past being taken from him. He only felt a new past flowing in, as they talked about little things in their lives, although their words were only straws, tossed about and let drift.

'I don't want to go in,' said Hannah. She kept opening her passenger door an inch, only to close it as the rain entered. 'Life's too short to pretend, my mother always said. She should have known. Don't you think we should be honest?'

He could not feel what he was shedding. Hannah kissed his cheek – then she had slammed the door, and ran up the garden path.

Back home, he found Miranda had left a phone message, saying she was going to be late home from work.

Thomas cooked dinner, daydreaming of Hannah. The phone rang.

'I want to see you, Thomas,' said the voice at the end of the line.

'Hannah?'

'We love each other, Thomas.'

'Han-nah.'

'Can't I come over?' Hannah asked.

'Are you drunk?' asked Thomas.

'I've had a glass or two and I'm about to have more.'

'Hannah, you can't come. This is my home.'

'I'm your home,' said Hannah, 'and I know how much you want to see me. You were thinking of me when the phone rang, weren't you?' He heard her sip at something. Then she said, 'Know what I'll do if I can't have you, Thomas? I'll kill myself.'

The long wake of the words withdrew. And she had hung up.

Miranda telephoned the moment he put down the receiver. 'I'm sorry, Thomas, but I'm going to be later than I thought,' she told him.

'Can't you come home now?' asked Thomas.

'I can't. Who were you talking to?'

'It was a wrong number.'

'Oh. I tried twice.'

'They rang back,' said Thomas. 'Don't you hate that?'

'Don't wait up. Bye.'

'Miranda –'

Too late: he had lied to his wife, for the first time. And the second.

The next morning Thomas walked rather than drove to the station. He scanned the railway platform, then the carriage. Hannah was every-where, yet nowhere. She would be sitting in a carriage of some other train, he told himself, the one already gone, or the next one down the line. She had not killed herself – of course not! She was staring out some grubby carriage window, knitting, reading, nursing a horrible hangover.

And she was a nutcase, he thought, as the city came into view. He should have known from the moment she answered the door wrapped in a towel – that wasn't normal, was it? What had he got himself into?

He walked from carriage to carriage looking for her, he could not stop himself, but she was not on the train.

That day he recalled Hannah's threat only intermittently, and as if it had been dreamt. He dismissed her call as drunken – she probably would not even remember it.

On the train home, however, he briefly felt panic. What if she had done it? Shouldn't he walk past her house, at least, and check for lights? And again he went from the back to the front of the train. But she was not there.

Walking home he saw a woman some way ahead, coming towards him. He slowed and smiled, before realising it was not Hannah – hadn't he glimpsed her in every street, every crowd, that day? No, it was not Hannah – it was Miranda, walking to the shops.

'I'm going to the supermarket,' Miranda, smiling, told him.

'I'll come with you,' he said, smiling back.

'No, it's alright,' said Miranda, 'but thanks. I just need a walk, to clear my head after work.'

It was the continual rain that made him miserable, Thomas told himself. Stepping into the shadows by the train station after work the next evening, he almost bumped into Hannah, who drew back.

'Let's walk together,' he offered, and found, to his dismay, he had almost added the word 'darling'.

They moved away from the station in step, past the little weatherboard homes. He smelt roses along the path.

'I wish you hadn't called me at home the other night, Hannah,' said Thomas. 'I've been so worried for you.'

'Have you?' she asked. 'Why?'

'Why do you think? Don't you remember what you said?'

Hannah bit her lip, and something very old unravelled in Thomas.

'I'm sorry,' she muttered, as they stopped under a streetlamp, the pearls of rain visible overhead in the mauve light. 'But I meant what I said: I will kill myself if I cannot have you.'

'That's blackmail, Hannah.'

'It's love, actually.'

Baby raindrops perched in her hair. He passed his palm over her head, recalling its shape. Her eyelids lowered. Then, ducking forward, like stepping from the platform onto the train that takes you to another country, they embraced. People leaving the next train began passing, clearing their throats, the soles of their shoes clacking the path.

'Let me put up my umbrella,' he said, stepping back, gasping.

She was crying and laughing by turns as they walked, he nursing her arm: 'I *will* do as I say,' she intoned, 'I will. I'm sorry! It's only the truth. You are all I have.'

They stopped at Thomas's driveway.

'Here, take this,' he said, giving Hannah his umbrella, before walking quickly into his house.

He found Miranda staring out the kitchen window, her hands in the dishwater.

'There's a strange woman in the rain, Thomas,' she said, 'looking at our house.'

He watched his wife peering out the window.

'She must be a nutter,' said Miranda, shaking her head, and looking down at the sink. He looked down too. When they looked up again, Hannah had gone. Miranda had not recognised the umbrella.

He answered the phone an hour or so later, only to drop it. The receiver jumped and twitched above the floor. He could hear Hannah's tiny voice calling, repeating his name down the line. Miranda was approaching from another room. He put the phone back on its hook, and stood by it. But it did not ring again.

At midnight, after Miranda had been asleep for some hours, Thomas walked around the block. It was cold. Long drifts of wood smoke hovered in the limbs of the gum trees. The path was still wet, yet the stars were bright. He saw the clouds had cleared.

The second time he passed Hannah's lightless house, he went back, and approached the darkness of her front door. His skin seemed to contract and prickle, and his hair felt strangely thick and tingling, as he realised the door was slightly ajar. Calling her name softly, he pushed the door open.

The house was silent, very dark. Thomas stood a long time in the doorway. The place felt empty. At last he moved in, pausing after every step, listening, feeling the wall for a light switch. Gradually he made out something blockish at the end of the hall, something with a living density and mass. Hairs started rising on his arms and scalp. At last his hand encountered a light switch, he turned it on – and saw only a chair before him, merely an empty chair, with his opened umbrella standing on it.

He turned on every light in the house, even the outside ones. The place was empty, and Hannah had gone.

Eternal Rose

My grandmother was the keeper of the music in the family. All musical authority devolved to her. Through her training and prowess at piano, her undisputed critical judgement and her regular attendance to concerts, her musical pre-eminence among us was unassailable.

She lived in a sprawling old warren of a house, where, apart from the introduction of a television, it seemed very little had altered in decades. Sometimes, as a young undergraduate, I would sometimes stay at her house overnight, which was closer to the campus than my home. One night, as I sat down to eat the dinner the old lady had prepared, I happened to mention the unusual house across the road – a low-lit, mock-Gothic house with an overgrown garden.

'Oh, the Isaacs live there,' said my grandmother, 'or used to. I suppose it's been years since they moved. Five or six years, perhaps … no, probably more than ten, actually. Closer to twenty, come to think of it. Sad story.'

'What's the story?' I asked, munching on one of the cutlets that were among my grandmother's specialities.

'Benji,' pronounced Grandma.

She wiped her little lips with a serviette so starchy it preserved its shape when she replaced it on the table.

'Benji? Who's Benji?'

'Benji,' said Grandma, sipping from the glass of whisky never far from her hand any time after mid-morning, 'was their boy.'

'Whose boy?'

'The Isaacs's boy – the family who lived across the road in that house you noticed. Lovely boy. Benjamin Isaacs. Oh, he used to pop over all the time. Loved the kids. He was so good with them.'

'The kids?'

'My girls – your mother and her sisters. Benji was only fifteen, sixteen or seventeen, and mine were just little kids. But he had a way with them. He was our babysitter. Benji.' My grandmother repeated the boy's name, as if savouring the sound of it, and poured some vinegar sauce onto her cutlet. Everything she ate or drank was sour, bitter or tart – pickled onions, blue cheese, pleated lemons. Even her tea was so strong it constricted the throat. I thought she had finished with Benjamin Isaacs. But she returned to him: 'Yes, Benji – beautiful boy. Champion runner. Unassuming. Sad story.'

'But what happened?'

'Oh, Benji joined the air force. In the war. Killed on his first flight over Germany. Yes. Eighteen, he was, or said he was. I think he was a year younger. They put him in a bomber. He was the tail gunner. Least-popular place to be on those big bombers, they say. So that's where they would put the new chaps.' The old lady folded and unfolded her self-supporting serviette. 'Yes, the chaps on the ground used to get a hose out when they saw the bombers returning from a mission. Get ready to hose out the mess in the tail gun. He was dead by the time they got him home, crouched in a shattered glass box, they said. Cold. Benji.'

She dabbed her lips.

'I'd never heard of Benji before,' I said.

'No, well – everyone lost someone in the war, you know. After Benji died, Mrs Isaacs never left the house. Not once. People thought she'd died. But she hadn't died – she just never left the house. I saw the curtains move sometimes, or a door close. The garden got overgrown. Before the war they used to come to the concerts and sit near us. But not after Benji died. I invited them to things, but they never came over. Benji was their only child. Special, he was. A darling of a boy.'

I cleared the table. She crossed to the low settee, sat, turned on the TV with the remote, and put up a leg on a footstall.

Being twenty, I expected my grandmother to tell me things she would not have told me as a child. She rarely volunteered, however. Her attitude seemed to be that the past had no obvious utilitarian purpose, so why bother with it. I, however, was always sniffing about the past – something in me needed to unearth what had gone before. She divined my instincts, and mistrusted them, I knew. She knew I knew she knew.

Yet the past would come out, in spite of herself, or itself. It oozed out over dinner, it seeped out with the progression of weak whiskies to seek the room's warmth on winter nights. It wormed its way into the simplest conversation.

Sometimes, late, after many drinks (many *weak* drinks), after she had long forgotten my passing presence, my grandmother would navigate her way across her living-room by a series of zig-zagging manoeuvres, like a ship avoiding a submarine – from a chair to the mantelpiece to the bookcase – before finding safe harbour at the old German piano, where she sat. Then her nails clicked the yellowing ivories, as her stockinged feet struggled to reach the pedals. She always played the same few things – three or four pieces from 'Scenes from Childhood'. She inserted empty bars where I knew no empty bars should be. I had heard that, as a girl, she had played the piano in her school gym – jazz piano – while the other girls danced. Where had the jazz gone?

On the piano top sat an 'eternal rose', a bottled, oxygen-deprived red rose, a gift from one of my elder siblings given a decade before. Watching my grandmother's stooped back, so intent upon the clusters of notes and memories and the spaces between, I knew something long ago had broken this little shell. She had been put back together again, a little unevenly, but a workable reconfiguration. Perhaps that was why she had remained somehow childlike – she had been preserved in pieces by some shock. Some bottling had preserved my grandmother, set her in aspic.

She liked to watch television after dinner while I washed up. Afterwards, I might look at a show with her a short while, before I retired to read – I was always behind in my reading.

I remember one night she exclaimed at a drama we were watching: 'Ah! It's one of the Darlings, playing the father.'

'Who?'

'The Darlings, the theatre family. They're all actors in that family. That's one of them there, playing the father in that show. I knew him as a boy, but he hasn't changed. They all look the same, I know one when I see one. They used to live a few doors down from us.'

'Really? When?'

'Oh – not so long ago – when I was a girl. Fifty, sixty years or so. Nice family. All in the theatre – generations of players. Sad story.'

Ten, fifteen seconds passed. An ad break came up. My grandmother sipped her whisky. A green, plastic, clover-shaped coaster had stuck to the bottom of her glass, and went up and down between her chin and the little spindly drinks table.

'What story, Gran?'

'Oh – he died.'

'Who died?'

'The Darling boy. Appendicitis. Only eighteen. A year or two older than me. He could have done anything. Oh, he could act. He was the most talented one, everyone said. Appendicitis. He first felt it on a Sunday and by the Wednesday he was gone. Yes, he had taken me to a party only the night before he went down. We danced all night. Oh, we did in those days. A different boy every night, we didn't care. The very next day he went down with it. The Darlings. Fine family. Intelligent – with flare. Famous now, the whole lot of them can act. They make films mainly these days, don't they. But he was the real talent. Died of appendicitis. I saw them take his coffin out into the street. What a day – dreadful. I'd been dancing with him on the weekend. Then there he was in his coffin.'

The old lady spoke while looking towards the television, her eyes following the living Darling.

'Then we heard it,' she added. 'That evening. In the street.'

'Heard what, Gran?'

'His father.'

'Crying?'

'No, no, no,' snapped the old lady. 'Not crying – no-one cried in those days. Playing the piano. He played it over and over again, all night, all the next day.'

'What?' I asked.

'What?'

'What did the father play?'

'Oh – Chopin's *Funeral March*. Talented pianist, the father. The Darlings all were. He played it until the next night came.' My grandmother shuddered, and took a gulp rather than a sip – the clover coaster ascending, descending. 'Then he started again, the next day, on and on it went. Terrible. The whole street listening. Nobody stirring. Dreadful piece of music – the *Funeral March*, Chopin. Dreadful. Horrible. And the boy could have done so much.'

Later, lying in bed, I was returned from that place the far side of waking. Hesitant clusters of music were finding their way about the house. The phrases travelled softly through the unlit kitchen, down the late-hour hall, past the isolated photos and tentatively into the empty bedrooms – tiptoeing, uneven phrases that underscored the darkness, the corners of my grandmother's house. It was a funeral march – *the* funeral march, by Chopin, missing bits, played from memory.

New Sound Recording

The board meeting finally finished at six, and Paul had to rush from the office. He was getting sick of it, really sick of it – the assumed bonhomie, the veiled threats of the business world. Paul was pretty good at it. But there was more he wanted to do, achieve, feel. He liked to be transported. That's why he liked a drink or two. And that's why he enjoyed the company of women. And he loved music. He liked driving along fast with music blasting out the car speakers. That was what he meant by transport.

Paul was excited this evening, it was a special event, a one-off; he had booked a five-hour session in the city's top recording studio, and was paying to record his daughter's singing group. They were not a band – they were a singing group. The girls were close to his heart, all seven of them. The group had two fine lead singers, two more-than-competent guitarists, and all could harmonise. They had performed at school events, openings, parties, weddings, old people's homes. There was chemistry between the girls, it was one of those things, and they were at the peak of their powers – albeit an early peak, the first peak – and Paul wanted to preserve it before school ended and the group's older members went their separate ways. Or maybe not: maybe they'd stay together – perhaps there was a little business opportunity there?

The studio was in an old, grimy six- or seven-storey warehouse by Central Station. Paul was surprised by the proximity to the railway. Didn't the sound and the vibrations of the trains affect recordings? He had to catch a lift several levels, as if going to another business meeting, and found himself standing in his suit and tie next to a long-haired, emaciated man, who was clad in a creaking leather jacket and tight black jeans – a musician. The musician looked straight ahead, and slowly donned sunglasses. His apartness provoked Paul, who never let any man get above him: 'Are you making a new sound recording?' he asked.

As if conserving energy, the man did not move or say anything.

The lift doors opened. Where were the girls? They should be here by now, thought Paul, checking his watch. Miffed by the musician, he strode down an empty corridor past framed photographs of singers and bands with golden awards attached to their portraits. Ah! He could hear the girls now. He found them in a long, dark room, jumping about on vinyl sofas. They kept leaping into one another's laps and squealing in the gloom. Some of their favourite songs had been recorded in this very studio! Only Karen and Emily, the group's two lead singers, sat apart, in a corner, earnestly conferring over a guitar, shuffling papers, writing last-minute notes. Emily was Paul's daughter (although Paul of course showed no favour to any of the girls, other than what was natural towards his daughter … although it was hard to ignore that Karen was an absolute stunner).

'What's going on?' he asked Emily, after waving and grinning at the other girls.

'The sound engineer told us to wait in here while he set up,' said Emily, smiling up at her father.

'Did he now. And where exactly is the studio?'

'Go through the door opposite the door you came in.'

The studio proper was a wooden-floored, high-ceilinged space about the size of a basket-ball court. To the right of the entrance a few steps led up to a room bristling with electronic equipment; to the left a small glassed-in area contained a piano. In the large central space a man was setting up an array of microphones in front of a semi-circle of chairs.

'Paul,' said Paul, approaching the man.

'Evan,' replied the sound engineer, limply enduring Paul's handshake. Evan had the pale, puffy look of the nocturnal shift worker.

'Not late starting, I hope,' said Paul.

'Don't think so,' said the engineer, squinting up at the tapered base of a microphone. 'The girls arrived about half-an-hour ago. So we got going early, in fact. It always takes a while to set up.'

'I see. And what's that empty booth over there?'

'That's the "fishbowl". The lead singer goes in there. We'll put the rest of the group in the big room out here. Separate the sound.'

'Right.' Paul looked towards the partitioned-off piano. 'Maybe they could use a bit of piano,' he mused.

'Oh – they'll be using piano too, will they?' asked Evan.

'I'm sure they could do.'

At first, in their excitement, the girls were squeakily breathless and out of tune. Paul shook his head: 'No they can do better, much better than that,' he muttered. He was sitting in a swing-chair beside Evan in the 'console room'. Evan perched before an enormous tilted board covered with rows of buttons, knobs that slid up and down long grooves, and fibrillating red and white needles. Together the men peered through a large pane of glass at the girls arranged on the arc of chairs. Only Karen was not visible; she was hidden in the fishbowl, singing the lead vocal.

Evan hit a switch that allowed him to communicate with the girls beyond the soundproof glass.

'Just relax, girls,' he said.

The girls giggled. They were heard settling, bumping mikes, apologising. Papers loudly rustled and slid. Karen began faintly singing.

'Did you record that?' asked her disembodied voice, growing abruptly loud and close as Evan adjusted a knob.

'No. I'm still setting up the tape. So relax, girls. Just sing a bit more.'

Paul saw the engineer glance at the clock.

The girls practised; one wanted to rehearse her harmony over and over; another girl said she needed to rehearse *her* harmony. Then followed a discussion about the order of songs. A last-minute decision was made to drop a song from the set list – at this one of the girls protested (she had co-written the song). The group talked as if unaware that Paul and Evan could hear everything they said from the console room.

Evan seemed to be taking a long time attaching a large spool to a machine.

'What's that?' asked Paul.

'That's the recording tape.'

'How does it work?'

'It goes round and round.'

'I can see that.'

'Oh, how does tape work?' said Evan. 'It's magnetic.'

'I see.'

'Don't ask me how magnetism works. It just does.'

Evan was watching the two circling spools, listening to the apparently silent tape. No: it did faintly hiss.

Satisfied, Evan pressed on the intercom button: 'Shall we do a take, girls?'

'I'm sorry – what's a *take*?' asked Emily.

'That's where you sing the song and I record it.'

'Oh! Yes, let's do that.'

'When you're ready,' said Evan. 'Can you all hear me?'

Seven high voices chorused 'Yes!' One girl could hear too well – it was rather painfully loud, she politely informed Evan. Evan turned a dial anticlockwise.

'Just relax, girls,' he repeated.

At last they were being recorded. After a few false starts, the girls got into a song. Paul was craning forward now. He had taken off his jacket and loosened his tie.

'Can I speak to them?' he asked Evan at the end of the song.

'Go ahead.'

'That's good, girls,' said Paul. 'But I think you can do it better.'

All the girls agreed they could. Yes, much better. Could they do it again? Of course, said Evan. Do it as many times as you want, he said. He could always wipe the tape. One girl corrected a second girl's phrasing. A lone voice piped in the static, electric silence, practising a part, a voice in the process of memorising.

'Do they want to come back to this one?' floated Evan.

'No, no,' said Paul, 'they've almost got it. It was starting to sound right. You wait. When they click, they click.'

'From the top?' asked Evan.

'I'm sorry – what does *from the top* mean?' enquired Emily.

'That means do you want to start the song again from the beginning?'

'So – we just sing again now, do we?'

'That's it,' said Evan.

'The whole song?' Emily asked.

'All of it.'

'From the beginning?'

'Yes.'

The girls began to respond well to the recording process, and in their enthusiasm soon had three songs 'down'. What did 'down' mean? It meant recorded. The three songs were sung by Karen, the group joining on the choruses, different girls taking turns to harmonise.

'It's sounding fantastic,' said Paul, taking off his tie – the girls were being caught in flight, this was making memories. 'Can I smoke in here, Evan?'

'Sure can,' said the sound engineer.

'What's this do?' asked Paul, fingering a switch.

'I wouldn't touch that,' said the engineer quickly.

The girls were now chatting excitedly among themselves, on a roll.

The fourth song, however, presented difficulties. They had to start it four or five times, and Karen's voice began to fray.

'A rest?' suggested Evan.

The thirsty and hungry girls poured from the studio into the room they had occupied earlier, praising one another, shrieking at the silly questions they'd had to ask the engineer, slipping off each other in the lather of the entire experience. At least four crowded into the studio toilet.

Paul was pleased to discover that the kitchenette contained a bar-fridge. Best of all was a bottle of not cheap whisky left on the bench, with a sticker over the label, which read, 'In Tune, On Time'.

The girls were confident and precociously slick in the second session. Karen nailed her last number, then Emily sang lead vocal on four more songs, hardly missing a note.

'That's my daughter,' said Paul.

'Sweet voice,' said the engineer.

They pushed on to the last few songs on their list: but some of the girls were beginning to tire and sing flat, and they began making less effort to be polite to one another.

'Time for just one more, girls,' said Paul, 'we're almost there now.'

Karen returned to the spotlight to cover an old favourite.

'Cripes, it's better than the original,' said Evan at the end of the take.

'Isn't it!' agreed Paul.

'That was very, very good, Karen,' said Evan. He was learning their names.

'I can do it better,' said Karen's also lovely speaking voice, rounded, disembodied.

'Better than that? No. Really?'

'How would you like me to do it, Evan?' Girls were giggling; the end was in sight, and the session was turning into a kind of party, on tape.

'I'll leave that up to you.'

'But you're in charge,' said Karen, 'of the session. Should we do it once more?'

'Um, er—

'Tell me what to do, Evan, and I'll do it,' said Karen.

'I think you've done just fine.'

'You're only saying that, Evan.'

'No, really.' Evan raised his eyebrows.

'Do they train you to say that at sound engi-neering school?'

Evan began sweating. He pressed the intercom off. 'Crikey, that one's a bit of a siren,' he muttered to Paul. Then he looked up quickly: 'But she's not your daughter, right?'

Paul cleared his throat and shook his head.

Karen sang the song once again. Yes – an even better performance!

The emaciated musician from the lift had slipped uninvited into the console room (he was invested with the authority, apparently) and stood listening to Karen with a distracted air, his jacket creaking.

'May I meet her?' he asked softly – quite impeccable, thought Paul. Surprising.

While the girls were packing up and Evan began a 'quick mix' of the songs (sounded like cooking to Paul), Karen slipped out into the corridor with the musician. The other girls, sitting about listening to the songs being played back, blushed at their triumphs, and wrung their hands and profusely apologised at their every imagined mistake. Too late now, it was on tape and in the mix.

Karen, red-cheeked, returned to the console room as the other girls were preparing to leave.

'I'm rehearsing songs with him,' she informed them quietly, wide-eyed. The girls gasped. One of them even had the musician's last record.

At last the engineer placed a single tape in Paul's hand, a cassette the same size but heavier than a regular tape. They all squeezed into the lift together, except Karen, who assured them she would catch a train home later – yes, yes, she always caught the train home at night, she lived on the main line; or she could always call her mum, no matter what time.

A few tired-looking parents waited for their girls in the ground-floor foyer.

Paul listened to the tape at high volume in the car as he drove home with Emily. He could not believe it – there it was, the seven songbirds set in aspic.

Halfway home, however, his elation abruptly flagged. He had secured the music, yes – but what about Karen? Wasn't he responsible for her? He had been so excited at the end of the session, and possibly a little befuddled by the 'In Tune, On Time' whisky. He'd had a few whiskies earlier in the day, too.

Well, the girl was almost eighteen; although that comment about the siren began to nag;

but the engineer was a harmless type, surely – a queer, almost certainly.

It was the leather-clad musician he worried about.

Ah well, Karen was the type who sailed through.

Any way you looked at it, a seductive business, this new sound recording.

The Tree Line

Autumn is coming, and you always return with it. When I am about to walk on, something stops me – it is autumn coming. I have felt the unexpectedly cool breeze on my face, and think it is you, touching my skin. I am about to step through a door, as I have a thousand times before, when suddenly I linger: I have felt the autumn.

I pause in the washing up, and lift the kitchen window higher.

Our home now is in the tree line beyond the yard; framed in the window, I keep the pines in my eye's memory, and return to the washing up. Evening is coming on, and in the pines, everything takes a step closer – you come closer – although I am stuck in this other place and other time. We step in and out of the trees, frightening the birds that had forgotten us while we remained so still. In the tree line everything is several degrees cooler and darker and less certain, the quality of sound is muffled and clothed, and the world beyond appears altered.

I scrub a pot in frustration; I am hardened into another form now. Back there, my eyes were not blue, and my skin not fair. I did not sing – or not like I must now. Even then, in that other time, when we were free to speak and touch, we were changing. Yet at some point in our changing, our paths crossed, and that moment set, and became fixed, outside time. Something met and hardened, and that point remains, like an outcrop of amethyst in the heart's core, in the heart's muscle memory. Our meeting is unchangingly adamantine to me.

I rinse the pot and place it on the rack to dry.

To the side of the kitchen window grows a claret ash tree, obscuring the road; its leaves have turned auburn and claret and golden by the barrowful. Most of the leaves are on the ground, but a few still cling to the branches. In autumn, the spaces between things grow as leaves are shed. The tree line, however, stays dense. An unchanging place, it stays green-lit and dark. And if I venture in, I will always find you again. Once inside, I can still hear the train in the distance, running distinct. It was not a sinister sound then, it merely signalled the changing times. We lived on the outskirts of our town, in a cottage on the forested edge of a field. Along the far side of the field ran the train, its carriages passing before picket fences, the engine and each carriage progressively blocking out the town beyond; it ran on under a line of lampposts, each lamppost turned at the top like a shepherd's crook. The field between was ploughed dark in spring, and lay snow-covered in winter.

When I first saw that train, we had just married. We were free to love. We worked through the shortening days in a vegetable patch beside the cottage. In the evenings, or, later, in the rain or snow, I turned wood to make chairs, simple cabinets and tables. You did bookwork in the town by day, and made and repaired clothes by night. We cooked and cleaned together, and tended chickens kept in a wood and wire run.

I remember crossing the field before the cottage, and making my way along the train line. At some point I became more floating than walking. The houses became closer together, and the gardens more compact. Short paling fences ran between the homes. The train approached – not sinister, yet still a wonder. Evening darkened as I floated on over the tracks and the rooftops. In one of those houses, in one of those streets, we touched, we kissed, we fell into sleep. Then the roofs were under low cloud, cloud mixed with smoke from the wood fires. I lingered above, before turning to follow the rail line back. The cottage stood in the distance, and I made towards the trees behind it.

Wind turns the pine needles, and I know I am stuck in another world, and another time. Yet I only need to open this kitchen window, and smell the resin and hear the wind in the needles, and I am back with you before the war, when railway tracks were not unthinkingly cruel, and the streets were not deserted in fear. And when I cannot reach that place, I must resort to words – in this life I have created a web of words, to lead me back. I sing of the tree line and us in that other time, and I return and we return in melody. I can sing you up. I can sing up the old cottage, and the potatoes and the beans, the chicken eggs, the lint and the wood shavings. I can sing your clothes, your smile, your eyes, your poised needle, the firelight flickering on your cheekbones, the light that gave your body form. Any time I sing our song – divided into a hundred fresh songs though it may be – time's scars soften and slacken a little, and what is left is our story.

I can sing in this life. Back then I had no particular voice in my happiness. I sang as I might laugh, or love, and did not think much of it.

Once, in the time before I knew you well, I saw you standing with the other girls at the edge of your village at dusk. You sang to the girls of the next village, who stood gathered over the fields to receive your song. And so the song went on, over the hills and through the dusk, growing thinner and fainter in its far-reaching.

The next year your family moved to town. One cold day I saw you stepping on brown stones that crossed a muddy street. You clutched to your side books of different colours, and wore a white scarf about your head. You turned down a narrow lane. I followed, to see where you lived – a blue house with a run of grey cobblestones before it. I would come to know that house, I was sure; and when at last we really met, I knew even then, we would live in a cottage on the edge of town, against the tree line.

Our time together was only an interval before the war. And when I returned to our home under the pines, after the war's duration, for a moment I was not sure I had found the right place. I had walked a long time before I met and followed the railway line. Although destroyed in places, it led me eventually to our town. And yet I doubted it. For only pocked walls remained, oddly isolated and at unfamiliar angles to one another. Abandoned, scattered vehicles, some burnt out, remained suspended and stuck where they had baulked at street corners, or were tilted half off the road – cars with their doors hanging, armoured vehicles with their traps flung open. Buildings had been flattened, some streets had vanished. No signs remained, and no-one was about.

I passed above newly dug ditches along the train tracks, until I recognised the row of pines, and crossed the field, now weedy and pitted. Our cottage remained intact, yet seemed closer to the railway line. I suppose it was because the field was unploughed and overgrown. Or perhaps it was because a belt of timber had been cleared behind, and the forest's edge had receded. The place had been recently inhabited, although not by you, I could see, but by men, perhaps soldiers. No trace of you remained.

I will make another chicken run, and another vegetable garden, I kept telling myself – similar thoughts had long sustained me during my years away – *and I will start to make things again. There is still wood in the forest.*

I had been salvaging tools from empty buildings and vehicles. Only that day, coming through town, I had spied some handy lengths of timber lying in what remained of the rail yards. And it was some hours later, as I returned to retrieve some of these lengths, that I witnessed something I cannot forget from that life: your face, looking from the back of a truck. Your eyes were lifted towards the distance beyond me, yet you had recognised me in the moments before I recognised you, I felt sure, and this slow knowledge burned down into me, and it keeps going, and going, like a cinder eating through lifetimes and generations. You would have turned away, if you'd had space, but you stood pressed by the surrounding women against the bars at the back of the truck. Only those iron bars kept you from falling onto the road. There must have been forty of you on the back of that truck, each with a shaved head.

Later, lighting the fire in the cottage, alone in the place for the first time, I wondered if it really had been your face on the truck. Without hair, faces lose particularity, and you, or your likeness, had been lately exposed to the frost and sun, and had coarsened. Something inside you had coarsened as well, beyond recognition – or almost. Every woman in the back of the truck had looked the same, hadn't they?

Yet it was you, I knew.

As I fed the fire, I would have hated myself, if that capacity had remained in me, for I knew I was not going to ask after you. I was not going to follow, or claim, or attempt to save you. I would have hated myself, too, for something seemingly trivial – that I found you physically repugnant in that moment. How could I have betrayed you so grossly, after wanting you through the years? It was the last thing I expected. The cottage still stood, the fire I had made in the fireplace burned again, I could still feel its heat: yet nothing was like before the war – at least, not in any internal way.

That night, in my sleep, it returned to me that your skin ran soft as magnolia in facing parts. It was softer in my dream than ever it slid under any fingers, including mine. Very soft skin goes very much unnoticed, unless one brushes it. Magnolia? But there was no magnolia back there, back then. You see, things are getting muddled and mixed.

My laughter is sounding bitter in my ears; I turn a cup upside down to drain, and survey what remains to wash up.

At least I can still perceive you from this after-life. Perhaps I see you more clearly than ever. I see you here, where the houses are silent, where the highway glides. Your memory throws shadows under the mauve and salmon street-lights. On the plain below spreads the metropolis with its x-zillion sea-lights. This southern sea and atmosphere have washed clean my sense of the past, and I see clearly the underlying bruises and cuts. In the days of general disintegration, you shored up your little citadel, ruled by your body, conducted by your wits. They called you queen of the village – a secret, tinderbox village. You held court in a little fiefdom in the forest, juggling the death-men – the men in black, who retreated and advanced and retreated again in numbers uncountable. The beautiful flesh citadel fell at last – how could it not; yet the shell of your body remained, to be driven away on the tray of a truck, after the war.

I assembled this story from the looks and silences, the glances and turnings-aside of the surviving inhabitants of the town, as inhabitants reappeared from the ruins, or drifted back in the weeks, months and years following the war. My story was no less inglorious (I could not have survived otherwise), but there was no witness to tell it. And what would *I* have done, I forced myself to think, if *my* people had been driven into the rain by the *feld grau* ones? I was even guilty of pitying the field grey ones. Most of them were boys, so young and far from home, so far from *Mutter*.

That first spring after the war the neighbours asked if they could till the field between the cottage and the railway-line. Yes, I answered, if you give me some of the food. And in return also I will make you chairs and a table, and I will build you a new chicken coop and paling fence. Although I knew by then that fences cannot keep out the main things – not even here, in this other life, in this other place, where fences are made of concrete and brick, and keys have codes. The past flows through them, jingling and jumbling free as wind chimes.

One night, not long after my return to the cottage, I sat before the fire with blistered hands, and cried: 'You don't own me!' I blabbed, not even knowing what or whom I was addressing – it was something ancient, something malevolent that had taken root in you, and, through you, reached into me. For over two years they had fawned on you and feared you, and you parcelled out your favours, the made-over girl from the village.

Now I can see you from afar, and now what you became cannot interfere and say how the picture should look, or how it should be. So I will say – to whatever you became – you don't own memory; or mockery, or intuition, or intelligence, or insouciance, or providence, or the sixth sense, or sexiness. And you don't own me, even if I did give you everything, and happily, before the war.

I don't know why the story only ever emerges with the fading light. The light alters – and the story turns and returns. All our days remain in the tree line, our memories and words, in indelible runs of feeling. Everything waits, ungarnered in the shadows. The shadows grow, and the story bleeds out, if only I open my eyes and my ears. I don't know why it emerges in this life, in this person, and not in the next or the last life, or in the next person. Perhaps it does.

It is taking me a long time to wash up tonight. It's taking almost a century. I fill the sink with more hot water, and feel about under the suds for any lurking knives, forks or spoons. I may as well be pulling out images from the dishwater, rather than implements. Things flash past in the glass. I see an old horse bow under the weight of a dray. The dray is stopped in the town square. The horse is blinkered, and stands resigned. Perhaps it is thinking, *No guns are firing at the moment, so that's good.* It is getting an unexpected rest, while a boy walks about the cart and drives a pitch-fork into the hay. The boy, who is in a soldier's uniform, pauses, and strikes, and strikes again, deeper into the hay. The horse stamps a hoof, for the flies have suddenly found him here. His ears turn back a little, as something begins to drain out the back of the cart. In the distance, perhaps in that lane running off the square, girls' voices begin to sing. It is a lovely day, summer but not too hot, and the girls are singing a melody not unlike the *Marseillaise.*

In the morning, three of the girls, or three girls, hang from three consecutive lampposts.

You would not have named them, I'm sure; but some claimed it was you who earlier in the day had gone to the officer, and told him of the pilot of the shot-down plane, the one who was hiding in the hay in the cart. But I don't believe them, they were only jealous of you, and they are always looking for somebody to blame, after the war. The pilot's body was revealed in the morning, lying in the gutter, plastered with hay and pocked with black holes. Everyone was too scared to touch him (or it). The message is always clearest in the morning, and strikes upon fresh minds, or, at least, minds at their freshest. Even now, I go into the morning with trepidation. For what message may have been left in the night – writing on a wall, a broken pot, a missing object, a hanging? Things loom too large, to much themselves, in morning light.

The top of the magnolia peeps above the kitchen window, displaying its almost insultingly silky softness. A little mauve perfume is released, and I am stabbed. It is unbearable what gets lost. The pink and the purple are re-emerging. And look here, in the saucepan in which I fried the chops, what beautiful shapes and patterns the fat has formed – those repeated, generic forms, which put in mind what runs beneath the material. I look, and can hardly bear touch, hardly dare remember.

It is not so easy, however, to forget you singing your future on New Year's Eve (it was a custom for unmarried girls to sing a prophesy for their life on New Year's Eve). That was well before the war. You were the last of the girls to sing. I wish now I'd listened better and could remember your song's words. But like the others listening, I was too struck by the way you sang it, and how you pronounced so harshly upon yourself; and I only thought of the sad, intent silence you produced in the room, which filled it entirely, filled it to overflowing. I do remember what you sang of yourself was not unambiguous, and certainly the news was not good. In that way, too, you were quite different from the other girls, who could only imagine and broadcast the sweetest and most promising futures. But your voice, if not your words, was smoothly textured and ran like light on gleaming blackberries after the rain, and that beguiled us.

When I encounter you now, in shards occupying different women in this new place, I notice none of those who contain something of you *sing*. Why is it up to me to sing for us?

Once, in this new place, while washing up, I heard music, a song that only we knew. I stopped to listen. You had sung that song for me. For the first time I remembered it in this life, and hurried to get my guitar. But my fingertips were soft from the dishwater, and the guitar strings hurt them. I walked to the next room to the piano – but in the interim discovered I had forgotten the song; it was stillborn, and I had parted with something of you, forever.

It is the change of season that ushers in the past – like a revolving door in the foyer of an office building, it turns, and we are brought face to face. You come to mind most strongly, fully intimated, in the first breeze of autumn. Invariably I am surprised; every year the southern summer solarises your memory, and for that interval I cannot see you.

Just before the war found us, I waited for you in our place in the pines, near a hut that had once been our trysting place. That was where we had agreed to meet, if – then when – the war reached us. You had left the house in the morning. Not long after, an unfamiliar-looking vehicle appeared, accelerating along the railway tracks. It rapidly drew closer, and I saw it was a type of tank. When it had passed (where was it rushing to?) I ran after you, found you in the town; but you told me to go back to the hut in the forest. You would meet me there as soon as you could. So I left you, to wait in the agreed place, listening to distant engines; and when I heard footsteps, I stepped from behind the trees, for you had come.

Instead, a man in a brown uniform fixed me with his small dull eyes. He was afraid, I realised. After a moment, he asked me what was I doing here? A plane flew low, coughed directly above, spluttered back to life. 'You should not be here,' he said. 'Haven't you heard?' And he led me away, into the town, into the mass.

I am sure you did visit that place in the woods, hours, even minutes after I had left. And in those first months of the war, when I shot to miss, aped those who knew how to survive, and avoided the ideologues, the military police and the crazy-brave ones who wanted to die sooner rather than later, I spoke to you across our separation, sent you word-messages over the rooftops, over the undulating fields and seas of trees. The words flew across the stillness and silence – and you spoke back. I would reply in moments between dumb action. Until one day, in a ditch, in full sun, my message hovered unanswered above me, un-received. Like an exhausted and bedraggled messenger pigeon, my words had returned.

In the corner of my sight splayed a hand. I considered its three grey fingers. You lived, I knew, but something had gone amiss, and now my words hung as unheeded as that dead hand.

I don't know why, in this life, I must keep trying to find you, over and over, in the people I meet. The cycle of flesh seems pointless, and something tells me to leave the flesh out. It is the vulnerability of tissue that betrays us. The flesh is the weakest part, everyone knows that. Yet it makes itself needed. I don't know why the inside of us is transported and wrapped in flesh – there can't be any better medium, I suppose. Yet spirit moves unsatisfied, kicking at its unsatisfactory horse and cart. You and I were climbing, climbing, climbing – then we felt nothing. Or you felt nothing. You became the hand that held nothing, thumbless and insensate. All our words rained to earth, unsupported in the silence.

At the end of our first winter apart, when the ice began to melt, I at least still felt something, for the melt released a fear of my imminent end. With the thaw the armies would move again, and we would be cast back into hell. But while we still skated on ice, we lived. And it was good to live, even in those days – perhaps most in those days. I felt most alive amid so much death. For, just to confuse us, the flesh at its most lovely matches any spirit or essence: to touch you again.

We first spoke while working in the town in the same cabinet-making business. You took the orders and did the books. I helped make or assemble the furniture. We began walking home together after the shop closed. Slowly, over the first weeks of autumn, then, in three or four days of burgundy and gold, we turned to each other. Suddenly my interests became very narrow. My future lay above your knee; now when we walked we began to share a sense of stealing goodness and happiness from the world, stealing eternity from time – as if we had stumbled upon a spell that suspended time.

Even then I knew something in you was beyond me. You possessed something intrinsic that was harder than anything in me. You concluded on a necessary action with a speed and decision I never could match, and you passed judgement more quickly and firmly. These differences in nature seemed trivial in our happiness before the war, however, and we passed over them. The hard things in you were barely felt in our combined spell, which softened and hallowed everything.

In the early days of marriage, while I was discovering the novelty of watching you wash and dress – all that – we slipped in and out of roles. Perhaps we played the parts of our parents and forebears. We even enjoyed bickering – I would become my father for a moment, and you your mother, or somebody else known in our beings. We would become aware of the play at the same instant, and it made us stop, and laugh with recognition.

We first heard of the war as a distant thing, something impossible to our happiness. We initially talked of it almost as a child's adventure, an event that must pass and which we would endure and outwit. Only gradually did its heaviness begin to hamper us. Then our words and actions became mechanical. We placed stores in the abandoned hut in the forest. *We can't hide from the whole world,* I would think, but not say it. You thought the same thing, and did not say it.

One night, I saw lightning reflected in your eyes; only it was not lightning. The following days we lived suspended, watching as the town emptied. Its inhabitants walked along the rail or clung to the train. By the third night, we might have been the last couple in the world. The train ceased to run, leaving an abandoned toy town.

The tank sped past on the tracks on our last morning before the war; I stood for some time unmoving, stunned. Then, with booming noises in the distance growing more frequent and louder, I set off towards the town to warn you. I found you alone in your family's new apartment

– it occupied the top floor of the town's single many-storied building, above the town square. You stood looking down through a window at the concrete street (no longer cobblestones for our high street). I remembered seeing you in that window from the street below, months before, when you had smiled down at me, before reaching up, your cardigan parting. As you had stretched up, the outline of your ribcage rose against your dress.

Now you were altered, I knew it immediately. The news was in your body, how you held yourself. Something had closed, something had turned. You stood with your finger pressed against the pane, directing my attention to a hole in the glass. 'Look, there are men,' you said, putting your nose to the window. The floor began to quake, as something tractor-like rumbled in approach, before halting out of sight. Then the building grew silent and still – if it were an animal, its hairs would have been on end. The apartments must be deserted – or the inhabitants were cowering. A door was flung open from the street, hitting the wall behind, and footsteps clattered up the concrete stairs, growing louder. Those approaching must be wearing hobnail boots. I could not remember hearing anything echoing from the stairwell before. At the gathering sound you turned from the window to look at me, and everything between us began to fall away in stages – some of it already had gone, in truth, only I had not fully comprehended until that moment. I had failed to see what lay distorted at the back of your eyes.

The boots reached the landing. I locked the door. The moment I did, the machine in the street resumed its clinking and grating, some primeval mechanical thing that had at last hit upon its destiny and purpose. Its turret appeared, not so far below the glass. Fear penetrated my numbness. The road was rippling like cardboard, not concrete, and the glass began to shatter around the hole, until the entire pane frosted. At a loud, peremptory knocking on the door, the pane fell onto the street, with a crystalline shatter. In the ensuing, highlighted silence, I realised the radio was on, yet nothing was broadcast; the dial was set on the government station, but the radio produced only static.

The men beyond the door called your family name.

'You can see it's me they want,' you told me, 'so go. Leave by the side door.'

I was confused. Our paths were splitting.

You could deal with them alone, you said, but you could not deal with all of us. So you sent me back to the house in the woods. 'And I will meet you there. Go, go,' you urged, moving to unlock the door I had bolted, while still displaying that red smile – you had applied lipstick, 'you must trust me.'

There remains a softness in me in your shape. Occasionally, women I meet more or less fit this softness. It is in the shape of what we were before the war. And there is a hardness in me, the hardness of hearing the last train leave, the hardness of being left, and then left again.

Our time before the war was really an interval between wars; we were also living *after the war* – that's how we thought of it then. We were the children of the survivors of the earlier war. 'Before the war' now seems a remote and discrete time, book-ended. Yet it finds its way into this moment, in the breeze, in that riffling down the sides of the pines along the tree line, in the discrete turn of their needles. It even cools the water in which my hands are immersed. And it blows through people I sometimes meet, the ones who are living parts of our older selves. What for me now is that other time of a time past, however, was already in your eyes, even from the moment we met. You had eyes from that earlier time. So do some people I meet in this life. I glimpse our past shot through their gaze.

I hear our past in some voices, too. How many generations are in a voice, and whose voice am I using, I wonder, when I sing? Our parents, or perhaps their parents reaching through them? And what other voices find their way in? I lay a voice over the chords played on the piano, and the two times are interleaved.

The black notes ring oldest. In them, in that other place, the river still flows, the grass still grows, trees throw shadows, and, where I waited for you, something waits still. The birds of the forest flit on stumps, and forage by tipping over fallen leaves. I waited there for you, and part of me yet does, thinking, *If you don't come, what am I to think? If I can't trust you, I don't know if I can ever trust.* When you did not appear, some percentage of me knew of all to come; yet the remainder clung to your final words, clung to images of you from earlier times. I remembered your hand in my hand. And even after we had parted, you did not let me go entirely, all at once…

Now I know how time gets formed: it is produced when one hand reaches out to another. Those moments – the little before, the little after, the baubles of possibility wavering between – form time. The future is forming even as one hand falls on the other hand; the future is still in mist. Then the warmth is communicated. One hand is always a little older, or younger, than the other.

When I was young in this life, I met someone who resembled you. Her eyes were as old as the world. On a cool, almost cold morning, when I felt alone and between places, she came up to me and laid her hand on my wrist. I recalled you doing this. I felt your touch down the ages. It was a little hand, and I recognised the bones in it. My heart paused. She led me to her friend – and I felt you following, if not leading – and my lungs began to breathe. I was born into our past life on that morning, born through several women. The sun came out, and the future fell untangled. Perhaps 'remembrance comes from heaven', but for me it is between heartbeats, when my heart has stopped a millisecond, and the life that I lived with you flows back. If I clear away the clutter that accrues throughout the living of this life, I am left with our outline. I run back down the cobblestones through the night to your door; I keep coming back, you might hear me under your window, where the flowers bend their heads to pray.

Every dawn I wake alone in this life. And when summer comes I mourn and even panic, for I cannot remember you, except in gossamer, or like the fast-disappearing trace of breath on a window. In the heat, nothing new is forged; it might seem as if something is, but it is only unthinking repetition. But with the returning cool I see how all things are forms repeated. With autumn foliage dies, the leaves drop from the trees, everything steps back into itself. The spaces between things grow, and sounds grow too. Perspectives are amplified, and the past flows in. But in summertime we struggle to imagine this return of the cold and what it brings, even if we have lived it ten, twenty or fifty times. Summertime fails to recall wintertime. Yet under the brightness the old things do wait, and with the cool they stir and unfurl. As long as there are seasons, you will keep returning to me.

Once I got soaked walking home from the train station in the rain. As the rainwater stuck cold to my goose-bumping skin, I felt you all over me. You leapt the gap, as the water meniscus reached between the material and my skin. Some people never wish to stand in the rain, to feel the return of what is held in the rain. They block their ears when the wind blows, they don't want to know. I would never know you – even if I do only cloak myself in your memory – if I didn't look out the window, if I didn't wander rain-struck. It is only when I forget myself, the way one forgets oneself wandering in the wet, that the other time flows through.

Certain trails of melody return you to me, and through the melody I find you again. Melody leads me to you, I sing it and I inhabit you. In melody's timelessness the current world cannot touch me, the here and now is like a skin I can slip off. The melody exhumes; up comes the past from where it had proceeded close under the surface of the everyday – like tugging at a type of shallow root, plucking up from under the soil the root's runners, one after another. I lift the song up and out, and the farther back it runs, the closer we become.

That harvest song of yours, the one you sang with the other girls in the days before the end of our little book-ended world – once I heard it here, sung by a girl on a train station. I turned my head, and wandered the length of the platform, hands thrust in my overcoat. It was winter in this part of the world, and the platform was open, raised and exposed. The song went on some carriage lengths. The past slid past – then I realised I had missed my train, and the song had gone.

I find a melody, it leads me in links to you; initially it is an unexpected melody, then I begin to recognise it. The unfamiliar becomes the familiar, and it returns a landscape to me, and situations in that landscape, and I remember us. The melody keeps us always young, always acting, and it condemns us simultaneously to great age, as in it we have joined the timeless conversation of the dead. We join in an old song.

Chasing this song, I am still doing your work. The chase and then the song erase me, and when I am erased most fully, I am most happy, being closest to you. Even before the war, when our physical selves were intact, and our life was that of a young married couple, so physical, I knew I was erased in my fulfilment, and that was happiness – until those things were taken away, and I had to become again, form again, and start to sing.

Even when we had known the war was coming, we did not hurry. We kept working. I finished a set of chairs, you measured and began making the curtains for the collective hall – you always had work, your family had done well in the recent changes. Then one night, inevitably, the war did find us. At first it was hollow thunder. You only lay down again. I think you knew: you could manage the war. The war did not frighten you. You were born to it. You would even prosper. You knew what was coming, and what to do. But you let me believe other things, because I had to. 'Haven't you heard the war is on its way?' people had been saying to me. Even the day before the front arrived, I would reply in my still-intact simplicity: 'We'll always find somewhere to go', said so often the line became a song in this life: 'We'll always find somewhere to go'. When I repeated the line on the last morning, you countered, with a half-smile, 'This is nothing like that.' *This is nothing like that.* I went outside, frightened for the first time, and it seemed to me monsters lay hidden just over the horizon; and over the trees giant inflated figures rose up to sway in the pale sky, rose like childhood dream-memories: *'Tomorrow's the day,'* they cried from far away in faint chorus, *'Tomorrow's the day you lose everything you've got! Tomorrow's the day all of the clocks stop!'*

That last morning I watched as you walked towards the town, over the field, along the ash path between rows of vegetables. Your skirt and coat were two tones of grey, and from behind you looked like any other young woman, unassuming. You seemed oblivious of the giant voices above as you went parallel to the railway track, your head down. You appeared most mindful of the future. I remember thinking, how could any harm ever come of you?

It was the set of your grey back and shoulders that made the war real. A feeling of imminent chaos and destruction has never quite left me. Everything could be gone tomorrow, I think, stirring the cutlery left at the bottom of the sink. Even in this other place, decades and lives later, the knowledge lies in people's hearts, and at the base of their spines, in the sediment of their minds – everything can be swept away overnight, or be taken between breakfast and lunch. I still picture your receding back; then images from before the war return, and I see you coming home, stirring a pot, or pouring tea. Images remain, and a story remains, a thread that is scattered and broken, yet identifiable still. I can track the trail, through the songs I still can.

I let out the dirty dishwater. The sun is setting, the last leaves of the claret ash are glowing.

Red was your colour. How I loved to look at you, and to hear your voice. In the first autumn of our marriage you gave me back my self. I would walk in the forest alone, if only to prolong the happiness of knowing I could soon return to you. Coming back towards the light beyond the forest, I would stand in the tree line, and watch the women pull a crop from the field, and pile the vegetables in baskets. To the low east, where the rail disappeared, fields stretched in belts of grey and blue, flat and far-reaching, until they met the low, white sky. Inside our cottage, in the firelight, the colours of useful things – jugs, pitchers, spoons, cups – clarified to richer, more enamelled tones of red, blue and yellow. I savoured the light on them. Everything gathered a ripened berry lustre, before the war.

In our second autumn, the only season repeated in our marriage, and not long before the end, yet more of my self was given back, and I had never felt so complete. I had never been so whole, or whole, before. My past had been lying in your flesh all this time. One night, we walked to the village where you had grown up, the place I had first seen you. We slowly passed the painted doors, the steep roofs, the small geometric gardens. Most houses had an outhouse full of sleeping fowl, and the birds cackled low, muttering as we passed. We neared the village square, where an old soldier lay in the gutter, the soldier singing a scrap of martial song over and over. A star fell. A cat tugged bones from a rubbish pile. Someone had once told me our relationship to God should be entirely personal and unmediated – that's how it was with you and that place, as we entered like spirits into the houses, and the houses entered into us. Unmediated. It was autumn again, and we could hear the train from farther away. For hours it seemed that train was rushing towards us, and we waited, not able to be separated. Then it blared through, and we were abruptly exhausted, and remembered we had to get up early in the morning, feed the chickens and go to work.

The houses on the town's outskirts shrank back a little as we returned past them. They turned aside as if in the knowledge any relation-ship we might have with them would soon be lost. In that moment we felt as old as the world, in our beginning.

It's time for bed. I clean the sink, having hardly had the energy to start the washing up tonight. Tomorrow I start work early.

There it is again, the next afternoon – the train heard farther down the line. I leave the station, one more commuter walking home in work clothes, a commuter with face down, intent on an inner world, shedding another day. I pass suburban homes, neat gardens, a blue-gum colonnade. Now the colder weather has come, the houses seem smaller, and set farther back from the road. The air is more clarified, and sounds have higher definition. It's autumn in the city. The world has expanded these last few days, and I expand with it, into a larger, older self.

Autumn releases me from the heat of this place. I cannot really think in the clotted months of summer, I can hardly move or feel – I'm snared in the present, I feel the whole southern continent is fixed in unthinking amber. But in the coming cool, the spell slackens, and I am released. I'm in no hurry to reach home tonight, as the other people seem to be. I stride a circuitous route, past the gums that stand so architecturally polished and finished. All through the summer they shed their skins in long slivers. Now I crunch their outsides underfoot. The world expands, and the past flows in. In those newly made spaces between the houses, hidden things begin to show. Beyond uncurtained windows people gesture, shift, speak; doors swing open and things are glimpsed and guessed. As the light fails, some rooms begin to blue with television glow, others are blocked-in with pink and orange squares. Words start to form in strings in my mind, they collect like beads upon a walking rhythm. Melody comes flowing along the opening pathways, escaping through windows, inside and outside. It's a variation on some old song we knew. Am I really the only one not hurrying home? I am already home, I suppose, as my home is in the walking, in the collecting song.

I pause before my front door, abruptly tired. The distance has passed in an instant, and only now does the exertion return. I turn on the hallway light, then from the still-unlit kitchen stare at the trees beyond the lawn. They stand so dense and black. Yesterday, the flame-red triangle of a fox's head floated then fixed a moment inside their darkness. The fox is there again tonight – I cannot see it, but I can feel it, watching me.

I find the guitar to start the song, the new song, which might be one of the survivors, as even at birth it already echoes.

While I was doing the dishes tonight, a fragment of verse from time past returned to me, a kind of cameo, and in it was the clearest image I have of you; *I saw a woman go down to the water, she took her time and she owned the place / I watched with the eyes of a fox from the tree line / And I felt the scene unfold in my inner life / I felt the way things feel on your inside.* The song had other verses with more images, which for the life of me I can no longer remember. But I feel that in losing them, I have lost part of you, of us, of our story.

I noticed, walking home this evening, that almost all the leaves had left the deciduous trees. In the cool of the evening I feel so close to myself. In these moments I fall, fall, fall through time, I slip into the songs. I begin to know us again, but I don't know how I know it. I know the face that is pressed to the windowpane, I know this road, I could walk this road again. But I don't know how I know it.

*I know the flowers in the box by the
window-sill, lie in the shade of the trees on
the distant hill,
But I don't know where that hill is
I know the shape of this memory and this
dread
I know the froufrou of skirts around the
foot of my bed
But I don't know how I know it.*

*I know your shape, and that's why I'm in
love with you
I know your face, and I know your voice
too
But I don't know how I know it.*

Previous Publications

'The New World' won the Bauhinia prize in 2001 and was published by *Idiom 23*.

'Children's Hospital' was published in *Things That are Found on Trees and Other Stories*, Margaret River Press (2012).

'Uncle Dan's War' initially appeared in [untitled] Issue Seven

'Vivien's Fingers' was published in *Review of Australian Fiction* No. 127, vol. 19, Issue 1 (2016).

Previous Publications

Biography

William Lane lives in the Hunter Valley, NSW, where he is raising three children. After completing an Honours degree in Australian literature, he travelled and worked in a number of different jobs. In addition to reading and writing, his interests include music and education. He has completed a doctorate on the Australian writer Christina Stead, and has had several critical articles on Stead published in literary journals. Transit Lounge has published three of his novels, *Over the Water* (2014), *The Horses* (2015) and *The Salamanders* (2016), and is due to publish his fourth novel, *The Word*, in September 2018. *Small Forest* was Runner Up in the 2018 Carmel Bird Digital Literary Award.

About This Series

Small Forest by William Lane is published as part of the Spineless Wonders Smalls series of small format paperbacks released to celebrate our tenth year in publishing.

To find out about other books published in this
series, go to www.shortaustralianstories.com.au

www.ingramcontent.com/pod-product-compliance
Lightning Source LLC
Chambersburg PA
CBHW030802190726
48285CB00003B/984